BREAKING THE RULES

Edited by Alex Davis

Published by
Boo Books
32 Westbury Street
Derby
DE22 3PN
www.boobooks.net

Edited by
Alex Davis

Cover design by
Emma Davis

Typesetting by
Pinnacle Ltd, Ilkley, West Yorkshire

ISBN: 978-0-9927285-2-6

CONTENTS

INTRODUCTION

By Alex Davis

What you're holding in your hands is very likely the first – and at very worst the second – release from Boo Books. A small press is something I had dreamed of running for a number of years, but anyone who knows me will tell you that I don't tend to rush into things. I like to let ideas rattle around a bit, settle, and then see how I feel about them. But running a small press was really one of those concepts that just wouldn't go away. So, it had to be done.

The initial thought was that I'd lean towards the fantastical, mainly horror and science-fiction, but as time wore on there was quite a substantial rethink in this. What I wanted to be able to do via Boo Books was simply to publish great books, irrespective of genre. I'm lucky in my line of work that I deal with a great deal of writing talent. What's more, often that talent doesn't have the outlet that it should have, that it deserves. Enter Boo Books. The rationale is as simple as that – quality writing that deserves its spot in the market place.

The other vibe that Boo Books has – and I use the word vibe to avoid using the term rule – is that of being local. We're based in Derby, a city in which I've lived for a number of years, since my University days, and a town I have a great affection for. It's a place that's been good to me, a place where I've got to know a lot of great people, and a place that has enabled me to pursue exactly the career that I've always been after – working in literature. So, in a sense, Boo Books is also about supporting so much of what is already happening in Derby, the East Midlands and the West Midlands in its wider sense.

On to Breaking the Rules, then. The genesis of this idea was actually born within a writing course, entitled 'Writing and Publishing an Anthology'. The concept behind this was that it would be an opportunity for new writers to get involved in a collection from the very beginning, and then be featured alongside a range of more established writers. It's perhaps an unusual way to put an anthology together, but equally something that fits eminently with what Boo Books is all about. So it's a generous thanks to all the attendees for all their contributions throughout the course, as well as the great stories they submitted. In this collection, they sit alongside exciting established and emerging authors from the UK and indeed around the world.

The concept of games being at the heart of this book was one that I came up with relatively early. I've always been an avid fan of games, whether it be computer games, board games, role-playing games or card games. So there was undoubtedly a real personal appeal to exploring this as a concept. On top of that, it's also a theme that can be applied very widely, and certainly has been within this collection. There are distinctive horror elements in Beau Johnson's 'Toad Baseball' and Allen Ashley's 'Queen of Clubs', which are counterpointed by more humourous takes in Charlie Fish's 'Death by Scrabble' and the wonderfully innocent 'Armitage and Isembard' by Natalie Perry. There are hints of science-fiction and dystopia in both 'Riot Season' and 'Players', which extend the concepts of gaming through to their logical – and dark – conclusion. 'The Forfeit' brings a fantasy, near mythic element to proceedings. This collection is exactly the kind of mixed bag that I was looking for when I cooked up the theme of games, so I couldn't be more delighted with the end result.

Oh, and by the way, if you can quite figure out 'Topopoly', do drop me a line...

Alex Davis
Derby, September 2013

QUEEN OF CLUBS

By Allen Ashley

Henry Merriweather had been playing Patience for two hours. He shuffled the pack again, flicking the edges of the two stacks and then gradually reuniting them. It had taken him ages to master this trick. At first he had been all fingers and thumbs but now he was as adept as any croupier.

He was somewhere around thirty; possibly nearing forty. Or maybe he had already crossed even that threshold. It depended on his audience: welfare benefits official, local council departments, potential employer or possible girlfriend.

He was seeking his perfect woman. He assumed that most men were doing the same. Some were seeking a harem.

His desk was the best item of furniture in his bedsit. Henry kept it neat and tidy. There were containers and a wire rack for all the necessaries such as pens, A4 paper, small scissors, large scissors, staples and so forth. A few years ago he'd obtained some home-based, pen and paper work, mostly simple accounts and book-keeping, but even that had dried up of late. The wicker basket by his feet was full of perforated newspaper pages. There were always adverts to reply to, of one sort or another.

He believed he was close to finding his perfect woman. But that was only chapter one. How to encourage and maintain reciprocal feelings in the chosen maid… that would be a much greater undertaking.

*

He awoke early, checked his post for junk mail (four pieces) and job offers, love letters and thousand pound donations from forgotten relatives (zero on all counts). Then he settled back down to a game of Patience. The cards still felt warm, as if they'd retained his life essence and kept it burning through the night like the Olympic torch. There were sour milk and stale cornflakes to consume, otherwise there was nothing to do except shuffle, deal and explore the pack until he could be bothered to go out and pick up a copy of the local weekly advertiser.

Both the computer and the TV were defunct; the corners of the room were either dusty or mouldy. He was a week behind with the rent and if he went out shopping this would drive him further into debt. There hadn't been anyone serious in his life since Sally. The newspapers were full of child abductions and showbiz titillation. His few books were dog-eared and overly familiar.

"It's just the usual modern male condition," he muttered to himself.

Even the playing cards were starting to show signs of wear. He arranged them all face up. The picture cards retained a certain brightness. As a child, he had often passed time arranging them into mismatched royal families and romantic triangles. The Kings were all solid, dependable types with worn faces and grey hair. The Jacks were moustachioed smoothies, lager lads who would inevitably barge you out of the way at a party in order to start chatting up your girlfriend. If you had a girlfriend. If you ever got invited to parties. The Queens, though… Henry supposed their attire was based on Tudor fashion and portraiture. They reminded him of a book he'd read at school about the six legitimate wives of his kingly namesake.

All the other cards were there merely to make up the numbers. The Aces were curious characters – simple foot soldiers but sometimes valiant knights in disguise. Four houses arranged in suits of thirteen. A court or a coven. Modern playing cards he knew to be a hybrid of earlier versions for chance and fortune telling, such as the Tarot. Sally had dabbled in reading the signs of The Hanged Man and The Wheel of Fortune arranged in different configurations, but Henry had always stuck by the cards more commonly associated with Snap and Poker.

He examined each of the four feminine cards in turn. The Queen of Hearts ought to represent lasting love but to Henry she was forever personified as the bossy frump in "Alice through the Looking Glass". Off with their heads! During one boozy night at a local pub, some guy with grubby jeans and a nose ring had told Henry that the Queen of Spades was considered to be the death card. The Queen of Diamonds was attractive but in this depiction overloaded with jewellery and, frankly, a bit tarty. The Queen of Clubs, however, was thin-faced, dark-haired, demure and serious. All the things he sought in a young woman. All the things Sally had possessed; but Her Majesty was, of course, blessed with a kinder nature and wouldn't desert him the moment some hirsute Romeo turned up.

The Queen of Clubs. His dream woman.

*

Henry was bleary-eyed from too much short-distance focusing. He needed a walk to stretch his optical muscles, even if it was only to the bus stop at the end of the street. He ought to buy some bread, milk and potatoes – typical bachelor food.

He looked at himself in the wardrobe mirror and had to admit that if he were sitting on an employment selection panel he wouldn't give such a scruff the time of day, never mind a job. He held up the Queen of Clubs card. There they were, together in mirror-land. Perhaps he should pair her with a photo of himself so that their sizes were more equitable. He searched through his desk drawer but the choice was between an unflattering ID card from Thompson Accountancy and several blurry poses with his arms tentatively around Sally. With the larger pair of scissors, he snipped one of these shots in half; but next to the pristine queen he seemed ragged and unworthy.

"Supposing she doesn't fancy me," he muttered. "What if she doesn't even like me?"

He would win her love and favour. Somehow. A task; a quest; an act of selfless bravery.

Somehow.

★

On the reverse of the playing cards was a picture of the House of Congress. At a glance, it could have passed for St Paul's. Henry had never visited America. The pack was a gift from Sally, lovingly bestowed approximately a week before she informed him that she was running off to Colorado with some Yank named Hank. Or Buck or Junior or something. Henry used them with conscious irony.

He had felt sick and sleepless much of the night. Every time he closed his eyes he could see plastic coated pieces of paper with red rhombuses and black clover leaves. There was a game he hadn't played in years, some form of Solitaire taught to him by one-time friend Billy during a rainy school journey. He split the deck in two, shuffled each selection. There was a "psychic element", as Billy had dubbed it, which involved focusing on a chosen card and attempting to extract it from the stack without looking. Henry closed his eyes, thought hard, harder still...

His left hand turned over the Queen of Clubs.

"If you really want something badly enough..." he smiled.

There she was with her wan smile and her Tudor clothes. Henry casually flipped over the top card on the other pile. It was the Jack of Spades.

The Queen of Clubs faced to her left, the Jack beheld events beyond his right shoulder, which meant that they were gazing into each other's eyes. Henry turned the clandestine cards face down again, shuffled both stacks, began playing the game properly. To his immense annoyance, the Queen and Jack revealed themselves concurrently a second time. He ceased the game, swished the cards around on top of the desk, and collated them ready for packing back into the box.

The Queen and the Jack were together yet again.

Henry hadn't spent this long seeking just to let some Latin Lothario barge him out of the way and run off with his all-time love. He extracted his adversary, sneered in his hirsute face, dropped him with dramatic deliberation into the wicker bin. Fifty-one was a nice number: three times seventeen. He was certain he could adapt several games to the new amount.

By evening, some of the jealousy had faded, to be replaced by a sense of unease. He tried shuffling the remainder of the pack and playing a game of "Elevens" but the cards felt recalcitrant and sticky. The Jack of Spades was still in the basket, his pride bruised but otherwise unblemished and intact. Reluctantly, Henry retrieved him. He warned the ignoble prince about his future behaviour, even waved the large scissors menacingly in front of the other man's face. Then he placed him between the ace and the two of diamonds.

✱

The Queen of Clubs was undoubtedly a depiction of Guinevere, most beautiful ever of English Queens, surpassing even Anne Boleyn and Jane Seymour. In which case, Henry was cast as King Arthur. And the Jack? Why, Lancelot, of course. Brave, bold, honourable… and treacherous. He would need constant surveillance. In the original version, a castle and eventually a whole kingdom had fallen because of the Queen's dalliance with her lover.

A very British dream had died, also.

✱

He'd been outside the flat for the first time in three days. The weather was drizzly and cold. As if he didn't already know, as if he didn't toss and turn every night in the draught from a broken window which the landlord refused to fix.

The local rag held the promise of a few accounting and stock-checking jobs but as prices rose it seemed hourly wages were mysteriously headed in the opposite direction. Still, he'd send off copies of his regular CV when he remembered to go out again and purchase envelopes and stamps.

Henry scanned the lonely hearts ads at the back of the newspaper. Several months ago, he'd dated a woman called Mandy who'd advertised her wares as, "Fun Loving Girl Seeks Good Times With Solvent Man". She'd possessed a pretty face and an infectious laugh but her ankles were exceptionally fat below her blue denims and she chewed pink bubble gum for three and a half out of their four hours together. When he enticed her back to his flat for a milky coffee, she started whinging about his lack of viable electronic devices, wanting vainly to check her Twitter messages on his dead laptop after her phone lost its charge.

They hadn't bothered to date again.

Besides, he was committed now to the service of the uniquely lovely Queen of Clubs.

✷

As was traditional, Her Majesty's image showed her face, clothed shoulders and bust down to somewhere above her navel, at which point the image was reversed. It was not a strict reflection, Henry noted, but in fact a rotation through one hundred and eighty degrees. Her eyes were blue, her clothing regal and in the one visible hand she clutched a Tudor rose.

He had never seen the lower half of her body, even wrapped in flounces and petticoats. Did she suffer a similar disability to the fabled mermaids? In which case, full physical consummation would be out of the question.

As if the rivalry with the lascivious Jack of Spades wasn't problem enough. As if class and culture differences posed no threat. Not to mention the dimensional discrepancy.

"My darling, you really are rather flat, you know."

But contrast was the spice of life.

Love could and would overcome everything.

✷

Henry found a tape measure folded inside a traveller's sewing kit. The logo on the outside informed him that he'd pocketed it on one of the very few occasions he'd stayed in a posh hotel.

All the cards in the pack were the same size but he couldn't put the figure into exact inches. After a minute or so, he realised that, despite the Englishness of the monarchs and the American patent on the reverse, the measurements were in the insidious, all-conquering metric system. Thus, each round-edged rectangle was nine centimetres by six. The picture of the Queen was seven by four. Allow a little extra for her unseen legs and she was maybe eight centimetres tall. The last time Henry had been for a check-up with his GP the top of his head had reached one hundred and eighty, which meant that he was loftier by a factor of twenty-two point five.

It couldn't work.

It had to work.

✴

He slept badly. Gradually, his discomfort resolved itself into a vivid nightmare. He was lying in bed, as now, with the slight illumination from the streetlight filtering through the threadbare curtains. He could just make out a figure creeping stealthily from the corner that had the mould… towards Henry… clutching a ceremonial but certainly lethal dagger… his wavy hair, curled moustache and red crown revealing the assailant as the duplicitous Jack of Spades!

Henry awoke, convinced there was a presence in the room. Slowly, very slowly, he edged far enough out of his camp bed in order to put on his glasses and pick up the large pair of scissors from where he'd negligently but fortuitously dropped them earlier. Suitably armed, he sprung upwards in a rush, chopped at the light switch, stood ready to face his attacker and defend both his own life and his lady's honour.

He could see no one. He checked everywhere that might have concealed a rat or a child of two. It had all been a bad dream.

The Queen was safely snuggled between the ten of diamonds and the four of clubs. The errant Jack was lying good as gold in the bottom of the box. Henry waved the scissors over the blackguard just to let him know who was boss.

However, he might be vulnerable when he returned to bed. There was a white loaf in a polythene bag in the kitchen. Henry sprinkled crumbs ritualistically around his camp bed. It was something he'd seen done for protection in a "Dracula" film. The bread should have been holy or blessed by a clergyman to really do the trick. It was a crisis measure, that's all.

It was a bad dream, that's all.

✴

The following morning, when Henry gazed at himself in the bathroom mirror, he seemed, and indeed felt, somehow less substantial. He had been unemployed now for nearly six months... and obsessed with games of Patience for almost seven days. When you've no job, no woman, no income and no real home it was no surprise if you started to lose your identity, too.

The Queen of Clubs was as placidly beautiful as ever. He held her next to his face, analysed their shared reflection, whispered, "Look, there's a place we can be together!"

But how to get there?

✳

He had become worried about shuffling the pack. Surely such rough treatment was patently unkind and disrespectful? The last thing he would ever wish to do would be to harm the virgin queen.

His refrigerator was virtually bereft of food. There was a quarter pint of rancid milk, a nibble of unnaturally green cheese and a lingering unpleasant odour. He'd finished the tea bags and the potatoes twenty-four hours ago. There was some loose change in the bottom of the sock drawer, maybe about six quid's worth.

Did he dare leave the flat? Would the Jack of Spades make his rapine move during Henry's absence?

He would take the Queen of Clubs with him, be her lord and protector. If she deigned to accompany him on his mundane quest. Was it fair, though, to shove her into his coat pocket or half-empty wallet where she might be squashed or even permanently damaged? He could cup her in his hand but what if he dropped her? The weather beyond the window looked chilly and rain-threatening. What might such inclemency do to her porcelain complexion?

And while he and her lovely Majesty were away, what if the evil, scheming Jack concocted some sort of palace rebellion?

He should have snipped the bastard on the previous occasion. Or at least have wrapped him up in a bin bag and presented him to the council employees on their Wednesday morning collection.

Again he held the Lancelot card over the wicker basket. A simple solution to their romantic rivalry...

"No, Henry! Please. For the love you bear me, don't commit such a cold-blooded act."

The voice was so soft as to be almost inaudible. Perhaps he was imagining it.

"Henry, show mercy, I beg of you!"

Sweet, lilting, unaccented.

Female.

He couldn't see her lips moving, couldn't be sure he heard the voice in his ears as well as in his head, but he dared not disobey.

Assuaging his vengeance slightly, he placed the Jack beneath a hardback dictionary. The burden of language should keep the felon occupied for the present.

*

There was a tin of soup at the back of the kitchen cupboard, behind a bottle of vinegar. It was a month past its "use before" date but would have to do for now. Even so, Henry would have to dash out to the Asian supermarket fairly soon and stock up on cheap and cheerful necessities. He would also withdraw the last few pounds out of his National Savings account so that he could visit Newmans the Stationers. Sat staring at the grey-green screen of his deceased television, he had experienced a sudden flash of insight, a way in which he and his all-time love might yet be together. But it needed planning and preparation.

*

It was hard to sleep at night after such minimal activity during the day. He would have preferred the room much darker, but the streetlight and the tatty curtains mitigated against this. His mind was racing, full of plans and hopes. Nervous as hell, too.

At last he plucked up the courage to swing his bare legs out from under the duvet, switch the overhead light back on and retrieve the Queen of Clubs from where she rested face up on top of his desk.

"Will you come to bed with me?" he croaked.

She was her usual demure self and didn't reply. He so longed to hear her soft wind-through-the-trees voice again.

"I'll be respectful. I won't force you to do anything. We'll just be next to each other."

Still she said nothing. No assent.

But no refusal, either.

She was shy, girlish, versed in royal protocol.

He lay for a long time unsleeping, with her unsullied highness held ever so lightly in his left hand. If he had propped the mirror by his bed he might just have discerned his own satisfied smile.

★

Eventually, he got up and returned her to the pack. It wouldn't do to be too pushy or too familiar at such an early stage of their relationship.

He didn't experience a recurrence of the nightmare in which the Jack of Spades had stalked his sleeping form but Henry's slumber was troubled nevertheless. Straining his ears, he was sure he could hear the fifty-two cards moving about… whispering… shuffling…

In the morning, he ran a bath, washed quickly but kept the radio playing so that eavesdroppers would assume he was still present. With all the money he could muster, he dashed out to Newmans Office Supplies and came back overloaded with best quality pens, pencils and a huge sheet of white card. He had enjoyed art and technical drawing way back at secondary school and had shown some proficiency in the subjects. Little good it had done him to date.

He began measuring and drawing, taking the utmost care at all stages. The glossy double-thickness card was at times rather unreceptive to his pens and colours but gradually his confidence and facility increased so that after about an hour the life-size depiction of the Queen of Clubs existed in ghostly outline. For the upper third, he had slavishly followed the details on the playing card. It was then a matter of extending her figure in correct proportions right down to the courtly shoes peeking out beneath the dress layers and flouncy petticoats. She was five foot six inches tall, thin-faced and slender-bodied underneath her regal attire. He decorated her outfit with stars, crosses, circles and geometric designs vividly expressed in gold, crimson and ebony. Correct flesh tone was the most difficult element to accomplish. He wanted her neither too blushing nor too pallid.

The whole project took him the best part of a working day to complete. Carefully, he held her picture in front of the wardrobe mirror to see what she and he looked like together. All right, the portrait wasn't Hogarth or Hans Holbein the Elder but his Queen of Clubs was a joy to behold.

"Soon, your Majesty," he whispered.

The longed-for alchemical transformation was bound to occur because he wanted and desired her so much.

"And what if she wakes and doesn't love me?" he pondered. "Ah, but I will do everything in my power to make it so."

There was the precedent of the Greek king, Pygmalion, who had carved the lovely Galatea out of pliable stone and married her when the gods breathed life into her delicate body.

"Soon, your Majesty," he repeated.

This time he really was exhausted and without clearing away his instruments he fell asleep for several hours.

★

He took a long time to surface the following morning. He could hear the saloon cars and the milk float chortling in the street outside. He'd have a major clear up today; smarten the flat as best he could in order to satisfy her Royal Highness. Maybe she had her own residence not too far from here and he would be invited to reside there in palatial splendour for the rest of his days...

He awoke, rubbed his bleary eyes with flat fingertips, and swung his aching legs out of the bed.

An awful sight greeted him.

His work of art had been scribbled over in black marker pen.

The Queen of Clubs had been defaced and defiled while her self-appointed guardian slumbered.

He wanted to shout, scream rage, smash, punch walls, sob, whine, end his useless existence and avenge her honour all at one and the same time.

The image was beyond repair, that much was certain. He slumped back down on the bed and began a wordless lament for his lost love. Just when it seemed this cursed life might become worthwhile after all...

There could be only one culprit. Vengeance must be swift and final. But meticulously planned and executed.

Against his natural inclinations, Henry dried his tears and prepared himself a stale sandwich as if intent on continuing a normal routine in spite of his bereavement. Minutes later, he settled himself down at his desk with a sugary cup of tea, collected the four Suits together, shuffled and began a slow, thoughtful game of Patience as if the world was still the same as two weeks ago. He placed them, covered them, reversed them, gathered them, put others on top – all as if this was just the usual business in the bedsit.

At an opportune moment, he picked up his mug and with actorly art-lessness also lifted the Jack of Spades. He hoped nobody else in the pack had noticed this secondary action.

In the kitchen area, he tried his damnedest to tear the card but the plastic coated wood fibre proved too tough. Throwing caution and secrecy to the wind, Henry raced over to the desk and retrieved the large, sharp scissors. With burning but controlled anger, he cut the card into thirteen pieces. To avoid any possibility of magical reconstitution, he flushed the remains of the evil Jack down the toilet, succeeding in disposing of all the bits on the fourth flush.

He glanced up at his face in the bathroom mirror. He was drained of colour, apart from his irate eyes that blazed behind his spectacles like the blue penumbra on a gas flame.

Back in the main room, he examined the ruined masterpiece. The reverse side of the double-thick card was reasonably pristine, having passed the night resting on the grey carpet. Maybe matters could yet be salvaged.

With some small scissors and his thumb and fingernails, he slowly and carefully removed the disfigured picture from the top side of the card, as if removing a painting from a frame or glass from a window.

The other side was most definitely usable. Fetching his new ruler from the desk, he again drew the rectangle shape with rounded corners, which would contain a stunningly life-like representation of his one true love. When he could face the task again.

He was shaking from the awful discovery and the consequent homi-cide. But the Jack had deserved it. How many chances should one man be given?

What if Moustache Man had allies?

Henry felt confused, tired, stricken with grief, and uncertain what to do next.

The rest of the artwork – a repeat performance of his drawing and colouring of the full-length, Golemic Queen of Clubs – could wait until later. He took her smaller depiction out of the pack, held her protectively in his left hand. Then he lay down carefully on the huge white rectangle.

"Nobody's going to cover it with marker pen this time," he affirmed.

He was so weary.

He closed the lids where the salty tears had almost dried.

He fell asleep immediately.

★

When he awoke, he felt stiff and immobile. He had a "dead" arm, which made him wince. To his left, he thought he espied the Queen of Clubs, but he must have slept awkwardly because he couldn't turn his head properly to check.

He had no further time to think about his cramps and his pains because in a sudden rush he was swept up by an apparent whirlwind, swirled around, cast against other people – overdressed strangers, they seemed – and finally thrown face down on a hard surface. He wanted to cry out in agony but no sound issued forth. He was out of breath.

He was possibly not breathing at all.

Without warning, a giant hand descended and flicked over Henry's minuscule body. Huge, bespectacled eyes glinted at him. Eyes he recognised. Belonging to a disturbed individual of his acquaintance.

Oh no.

He caught a silvery sparkle over to his right. Getting closer… wielded by the mad hands of the guy with the insane eyes.

The approaching apparition opened its sharp mouth above Henry's prone flat form.

UNEXPECTED MOVE

By Diotima Sophia

Quite why people expect me to enjoy a game of chess, I will never understand. Yes, I am a reasonably intelligent being, and chess does require a certain amount of intelligence; to that, I agree. And yes, it does take time and, after all, I have far more of that particular commodity than one might think, to look at me.

But still, let us admit at the outset, that chess can be, and indeed often is, among the greatest purveyors of tedium that humans have yet produced. (It will be noted that I leave all televisual incidents out of the reckoning, here, not having quite ever seen the value in the entire enterprise). Humans sit and stare at a board for hours, and move the odd piece from here to there. They gain nothing but praise and lose nothing but pride in the vast majority of matches, so very unlike the reality on which the game was based – time was, losing one's queen really did presage disaster, and losing one's king really was the end of everything (generally including one's life). Now, it merely means that one has been bested in a game of wits by an opponent who generally offers no more physical danger than a moderately-sized poodle.

I do not care for chess. As, indeed, you may have gathered.

But I am, at times, forced to play the game. This arises either because I am beholden to someone who wants to play, or because I need to get close to someone who plays, or because I need to be where the game is being played, or because… well, you understand the idea. I play out of necessity, rather than choice.

It is an easy game to learn and a very difficult game to master – but then, of course, I have had a long time to attain mastery of it. I marvel at the small, compact sets that people now carry about with them so easily – I remember when chess (or whatever it was called in the appropriate language) truly was the pastime of only those who could afford both the ornate sets (often inlaid with precious stones) and the leisure to play such a time-consuming, boredom-inducing game. I'm afraid my feelings about the game will intrude throughout this narrative…

This particular game was being played under tournament conditions (so I was assured), in an old, ramshackle house belonging to another of my race. I had been sent to investigate some odd rumours which had begun to circulate about him, but of course I had not announced this as the pretence for my visit. Instead, I had ascertained that a minor celebrity in the world of chess was a guest in the house, and used this as an excuse to gain an invitation. As perhaps has become clear in these tales, I am not entirely unknown among my kind and even have a certain notoriety; mine host saw my sojourn under his roof as a bit of a coup and had invited others, vampire and human, to meet me. This much I expected. To be set to play the ridiculous game, I had not. I had merely expressed an interest in meeting the man, not in playing the game.

But such was the plan my host put into action, and such was my need to continue to observe him, that I acquiesced, all the while protesting that my meagre skills were beneath those of my opponent, that I would provide him with no challenge. It was to no avail. After what I was assured was a sumptuous evening meal (my host and I had absented ourselves on some pretext or other) the guests were assembled and the game was laid out.

"Tournament conditions," I was told, included not only a very standard set (I could see a beautiful, ivory inlaid set on my host's table, but we were playing with nothing more exotic than Chinese produced plastic), but using a timer. Each player had a set amount of time, which was shown on one of two clock faces on the timer. When each player finished his turn, he would depress a button, stopping his clock and starting the clock timing his opponent. Even the mechanism for keeping time was dull, pedestrian and, yes, you guessed it, boring. I was not looking forward to the night, at all.

✱

The old man who sat across from me looked simple enough – medium height, medium build, completely unremarkable. As the game progressed, I found another thing about him was unremarkable – his skill in playing chess.

Every move predictable – good moves, to be sure, but not good enough. Every move in more or less the same length of time – good times, yes, but not challenging ones. He was clearly thinking two or three moves ahead, but lacked the ability to do more than that.

Which is hardly surprising – humans can rarely do that kind of thinking, for a very simple reason: they are trapped in time. Trapped! They feel themselves to be so much the masters of the planet they infest yet they have not yet conquered the simplest of their bonds. They live, they die, and they experience it all through one simple lens – that of going one direction through time.

One could almost pity them… if one were of a mind to do so. I, of course, am not.

And yet, and yet – there was something different about this one. (King to bishop three – an intelligent move). There was far more time to him than was normally the case. (Bishop to knight five – a reasonable countermove on my part).

So – this puts my opponent in one of two camps. He is either one of the very long-lived humans. … But, ah, no. He did not join us at table, did he? He was absent, along with Gustav – "showing the new arrival the additions to my cellar" indeed. Dear Gustav, most of your guests have long since realised why they never see you eat, and I would assume that your "new arrival" is another such, is he not? And yet, still as trapped as the rest of your guests – experiencing one day after another, in an endless, monotonous tide, tramping past, one by…

Pawn to queen four? What does he mean by that?

I've been ruminating too long on vampires and humans – I've let him gain a serious advantage. This will not do.

★

By the look on his face, my last move had disconcerted my opponent. That pleased me, in an entirely unpleasant way. I disliked him – he was smug, self-assured and gave off an air of knowing far more than the rest of the company. (Whether he did so, or not, was frankly immaterial – I do not expect to be the most knowledgeable being in any gathering. I do, however, object to being told that I am a knowlessman in quite such a blatant fashion. I also find that the situation goads me to prove just the sort of thing I do know, which rarely ends well for anyone involved).

I had, however, come to the reluctant conclusion that a happy ending might be beyond hope, anyway. The rumours about our host were, as far as I could see, nothing more than that.

His chessmaster, however, was another matter entirely. There were no rumours about him – you can be sure I would have heard them, had they existed. And there could be no rumours about him; that could not be allowed. But I was still without some vital information.

To wit: did our host know just what sort of being he was harbouring within his walls? And more importantly – did I? I had suspicions – this was no simple human. In fact, I was reasonably sure it was no human at all. What I needed to know was…

Oh. I appear to be three moves away from being in check.

I moved my queen to his king's six, in a desperate attempt to draw him away from his offensive (quite, quite offensive, his manner had not improved) position, as this should force him to retreat to protect his own monarchs.

It also had the effect of allowing me to answer my own question. I had noticed up to this point that the clock seemed to move more slowly for my opponent, but until I understood that he was not human, I simply put this down to my incredible dislike of the game. But now… now I was sure.

His turns seemed to take longer because they were longer.

He was manipulating the clock. Well, no, that is not the way to phrase it. Anyone can manipulate a clock – you can set it, overwind it, a clockmaker can change the mechanism so it runs slow or fast. What my opponent (now extending his turn to the point others were in danger of noticing – that quick young woman, more intelligent than beautiful, has already checked her watch against the clock twice) was doing was manipulating time.

This, of course, gave him a measure of security – the watch on the arm of the young woman was within the radius of his influence and therefore would run at exactly the same speed as every other time piece in the room. And every other heartbeat, the pouring of the wine… It was all slowed down during his turns. Because he was a traveller. A traveller through time, or a time walker – most commonly known (to the few who knew) simply as a traveller.

One of the most dangerous beasties on the planet.

Think of it. A traveller can let you live your entire life (yours, not mine) in what seems to you to be years but to others around you (depending on how closely focused the traveller is on you) to be months, days – even minutes, for the very old and very skilled.

★

I did not, of course, join the assembled guests at breakfast the next morning; but then, they must certainly have been used to such absences. I feel sure Gustav did not usually make an appearance early in the day. In fact, it might be some time well into the afternoon before he was missed.

As he would continue to be.

Even travellers need to sleep. When aided by a very subtle suggestion on my part, that sleep can be quite deep enough. I am normally a skilled and very quiet hunter – you can be sure that I used every skill I possessed that night. In the end, it was a fairly simple dispatch. Travellers are not immune to the knowledgeable application of seven inches of cold steel. ...

Gustav was a slightly different matter. I had no hope of finding him asleep or even somnambulant. His demise – which took place in a far removed wing of the house, away from anyone who might – fatally – have tried to come to their host's aid – was a rather more strenuous undertaking. Though not so ancient as I, Gustav was not young, and therefore strong, wily and capable.

Thankfully, however, not as capable as I.

So, yes, I confidently expected it to be at least mid-afternoon before either was missed, and probably the next day before any systematic search was put in hand.

Good luck to it. There is very little left when a vampire of Gustav's age finally succumbs to the Grim Reaper. What remained of the traveller had exited the house with me, in a large suitcase I appropriated from its room.

After all, the original owner would have no further need of it...

TOPOPOLY

By Gary Budgen

Sometimes as I explore the forest I have a sudden outburst of speech. It comes over me like an attack of nausea, and I emit things I have no idea how I know.

"The branch of mathematics known as topology started in 1735 with a paper by Leonhard Euler known as "The Bridges of Konigsberg". In this paper the problem of crossing the seven bridges was presented. It was demonstrated that it was impossible to cross all of the bridges in the city crossing each bridge only once. Thus a real place became the source of mathematical conundrum; topography becomes topology."

Another day, in another part of the forest (and it is always another part of the forest), I suddenly say:

"The 1970s super-group Yes made an album called "Tales from Topographical Oceans". By 1985 it was impossible to get more than 50 pence for it if you tried to sell it in Record and Tape Exchange.

"Not that you sold your copy of the album. You would never do that because of the cover."

As I've said I don't know how I know these things. I wander in the forest each day from first light. In places it is dense, the trees packed together so tightly that it is a struggle to squeeze between them. The sunlight there is transformed into a dark brooding green and the heat is oppressive. In other places the trees are spread out, the light plays on open avenues and there might even be a light breeze. There are no animals here. Not so much as a woodlouse. The rations in my pack – mostly dry biscuit that I wash down with water from little pools – seem to be lasting indefinitely. I realise that it is significant that I have never passed the same area of forest more than once; it suggests I am moving through a set of distinct zones.

I have begun to classify the regions of the forest according type (some of which I have mentioned but will restate for the sake of completeness):

A = Dense badly lit areas.

B = Open well lit areas.

C = Areas in between A and B in terms of denseness of tree population.

D = Areas unclassifiable as A, B or C

It is D that causes me concern and I realise I must work a little harder with my classification. The D regions might be wide plains with barely a tree in sight, and so could feasibly be classified as a subset of B. Yet there are also areas of ferns and places where stinging nettles are scattered in great clusters. There are areas where trees have been felled, leaving stumps, splinters and dust on the ground; usually these areas look as though they might once have been type A regions (although they now more closely resemble type B). It is just as likely that they might have been type C regions or even that they were type D regions of a sort that is different to the type D regions they now are.

Then, today, I found the note. A plain white piece of paper pinned to a tree.

You have decided to play Topopoly. In one sense this is a simple game with simple rules. The simple rule is that you must keep going until you have discovered the true rules. These rules are not simple at all. Good luck.

Perhaps it is like a paper-chase.

*

This morning I awoke with a single word passing my lips. It changed everything. The word was "lumberjacks". Why had I not seen the significance before of the tree stumps? It is evidence that I have been acting on the assumption that:

Other people exist.

It is true that the note pinned to the tree might have led me to uncover this assumption except that for some reason it didn't. The note is much more a part of the world; a part of the rules; I could no more credit the existence of the note to an actual being than I could begin again to believe in a supernatural god because of the existence of the trees. The note just is. And I accept that. However, felled trees are evidence of other people and if there are other people, where are they?

I have been forced to reclassify. Regions A to D must be regarded as a subclass of a larger set (let us call it X) of regions that are without people. This requires the existence of another set, Y, regions with people.

I did not move all morning. Lying on my back in a spacious region B I watched the sun reach its zenith. Perhaps I intended to stay there, to not move on at all but I knew that would not be playing the game that I had agreed to play.

*

"You are a man who likes the forest," I said, "you like to walk in the forest near the university every morning before going back to your office and working on a problem or to the lecture theatre to address the students. You like the forest because each part of it is unique, each tree is unlike any other tree, and each leaf is its own pattern. Nature possesses what the poet Gerard Manley Hopkins called "inscape", a quality which affirms that no one thing is exactly the same as another.

"Thus you enjoy the forest because it is so unlike the work you return to when you leave it."

After I had finished saying this I realised that there were tears in my eyes.

I got up and struggled through a type A region, thrashing with my arms to clear a path through intermeshing branches until my jumper was ripped and there were scratches on my arms.

When I finally collapsed into the curved roots of a great oak I was exhausted.

I awoke and immediately moved into a type B region and said to myself: "You are in the Lakes of Wada."

I felt suddenly light-headed, happy even, not that I understood what it means. I have seen no lakes here, no bodies of water bigger than the puddles I drink from.

As I trotted along I began to talk:

"You once told your students that you had invented a game based on the Lakes of Wada. You showed them a projection of an island; in the island are cut canals of red, blue and green. Kunizo Yoneyama demonstrated this problem in his 1917 paper. He goes on to show that if you are on the border between a canal of one colour and a canal of another colour, you are in fact on the border of canals of all three colours. Later Yorke came to similar conclusions when plotting the fates of a pendulum, the places where it might come to rest. The fates are each plotted as a different colour... 'But,' interrupted a student from the front – she is a young woman, dark haired, attractive, you have some kind of connection with her – 'topological spaces aren't real spaces.' You held up your hands, 'You are quite right,' you said, 'that's where my game comes in. Now let me tell you about Topopoly. ...'"

All this is baffling to me and even as I begin to try to decipher it I have realised a number of things:

1. I know what dreams are.

2. I don't dream here.

3. These outbursts of speech might, somehow, be in lieu of dreams.

4. That this understanding, this deciphering is part of the undiscovered rules of Topopoly.

That (as the notice on the tree said) trying to understand the rules of Topopoly is--in fact--to play Topopoly.

✴

Or are sets X and Y in fact subsets of D?

✴

"'But it was just a joke, wasn't it?" the dark girl, who is now Antoinette, now your fiancée, asked as you both strolled in the grounds of the university, on the edge of the forest. You must have been thinking about something else because you didn't answer and she continued. "You said to imagine a Monopoly board where every sector is connected to every other sector, without tearing the board apart and gluing it. These connections must be achieved through folding following the operations of a series of functions."

"'Oh,' you said at that point, 'perhaps London is a bit ambitious.' You were looking into the forest and thinking about the set of aerial photographs you'd recently commissioned that now lay scattered across your desk. She squeezed your hand and you felt warmth flow through you for a moment. 'No,' you said, 'that wouldn't be at all practical, would it.'"

"'Well,' she said, an edge in her voice, 'it's the holidays soon and you can take a break at last.'"

✴

"The Yes album was terrible, self-indulgent twaddle. You preferred The Stones and The Faces. But the cover snared your imagination. The picture shows the surface of a world that was, as indicated by the shoal of fish, also the bottom of an ocean. In the distance the isolated form of a ziggurat, the sun setting behind it. The features of the foreground are mostly the smoothed surfaces of rock formations, topography caught at the point of becoming the formalised shapes of topology."

✴

For moments today I have been distracted by the beauty of the forest, the inscape that I am sure Antoinette once told me about; the way particular parts such as the edge of a leaf, the rough skin of a tree, can never be categorised.

Then I realised that this is not playing the game and that the only way to go on is to keep playing Topopoly.

✱

"You watched her drive away, her anger expressing itself in the way the car juddered, the way it had shown itself, ten minutes before, in the stiffness of her shoulders and the rigidity of her head as she left the room carrying the holdall. It is only a holiday you told yourself; she is not going forever. But you had argued because you were supposed to go with her. 'I have things I have to do here,' 'What things?' 'Work, there's this problem I've been looking at.' She had seen your desk, the attempt to fold the aerial photographs of the forest. Perhaps she even has access to your computer and the complex transformation of the series of co-ordinates you took on your walks among the trees. For a moment her eyes seemed to plead; then she turned away. Later that afternoon you went, once again, into the forest."

I said all this as I sat on a tree stump, where I still am. It is on the edge of an area largely cleared by felling; but there are, dotted here and there, odd trees that have been left standing. At the edge of the clearing the forest is thick, like a type A region except that the trees have a characteristic that I have never seen before: they have been coppiced. Each tree has three or four thick trunks from a point just above the ground.

This therefore must be classified as a type D. Since it is possible to pass from any of the regions to any of the others it is possible to move from one type of place to any other. This must include type Y regions (regions with people) which are a sub-set of D (possibly). Therefore it is a just as likely that the next move I make could return me to a place like that from which I believe I originated; a place where there are such things as desks, universities, such people as Antoinette.

"She never came back did she? There was a moment when you realised that, sat in your office surrounded by your aerial photographs of the forest, your charts of possibilities and transformations. On the wall was a poster of the Yes album cover and an antique Japanese ink painting of the Lakes of Wada. There was no photo of Antoinette and you now felt that as an enormous loss, as though possessing an image of her might bring her back. All that was left was your work but that spiralled out of control;

not in the sense of not making any sense but rather it is beginning to make sense of more things than it should; so that the slightest detail (the circular stain of a coffee mug; the lines drawn by raindrops running down a window) has assumed a significance that is ominous, all encompassing."

Later I wander through a region of scrub where saplings poke out from between a rocky, sandy ground. This area continues to every horizon so that it might go on forever; except that I know I will soon pass on to another type of region.

I realise now that something has happened to me, that my decision to play Topopoly was shaped by events immediately prior to it. But establishing a chronology is impossible. When I remember my life with Antoinette it might be eons ago, it might be a moment ago, and memories of being in the forest an illusion. What frightens me is that not only every movement I make but every memory, every word and thought feels as though it might lead to any other memory, word, or thought.

The only consolation is the realisation that I can play Topopoly inside as well as out, that a game has rules and a discipline that might somehow save me.

✷

"There were voices calling from the edge of the forest, lights shining as it became dark. Why are they looking for you? Why are they bothered?

"Back at the university the computer program reached the point where it produced its final transformation. The results were startling, astounding, and possibly meaningless. After that you tore the pictures off the wall, tipped the desk over. From the shelves you pulled books: your precious copy of Flegg's From Geometry to Topology, Adams' Infinite Loop Space; and your collection of the Journal of Topology. Everything was scattered across the floor. Dry academic prose burns remarkably well. This time when you walked into the woods, the glare of a gold and scarlet inferno reared behind you and you became a shadow before the flame."

✷

Today I strode with new resolve along a path through a type C region, the trees spread out almost evenly, and a helpful path winds its way around them. The sun is warm and there is a light breeze that is bringing freshness from somewhere. Perhaps that breeze is blowing from the Lakes of Wada for just as they prove that the border of any one region must be next to the border of all other regions so I conclude my own situation is open to the various interpretations.

1. I am mad.

2. I am in a simulation.

3. I have made reality conform to topology.

4. Reality has always conformed to topology and all my memories are false.

5. There are a number of other possibilities. That number is n where n is determined by the structure of space occupied by all the possibilities listed here.

Then I see up ahead something white, a notice pinned to a tree.

Congratulations. You have become quite the Topopoly player. You have discovered the first rule: that you are passing not only through space but through contingencies. It is time now to move on.

Beyond this the trees thin out and eventually disappear. In the distance I see the roofs and spires of a town, perhaps a city. It is not a place I recognise but I know that it will be divided into areas and all I can do is fathom its intricacies, its connections. All I can do is play.

KEEPING SCORE

by Jay Wilburn

"I've never heard of this game," Dan said as he reclined on the bed.

He eyed the two dozen roses in the silver vase on the desk at the end of the bed behind her.

Evelyn smiled, "My sister and I made it up."

"Hills and Valleys," Dan repeated as he loosened his tie.

Evelyn nodded. The top of her dress hung down, giving a peek of her breasts that Dan had only seen twice before their wedding night.

"Eve, playing cards is not what I had planned tonight, you understand."

She laughed and accepted her new husband leaning up and kissing her hard on her lips and then down her neck. "Oh, I'm sure, but we have room service coming and I won't be naked when they drop it off."

"We'll see."

He squeezed her immodestly and she laughed again. "There will be plenty of time for that tonight, and every night to come."

"That's what they all say."

She pulled back from his grasp. "That's what all of who says, Daniel Thomas Dorit? Do you have other wives lined up?"

"Stop, Eve. I just mean the other married guys say... nothing. Just pretend I didn't say anything."

"No, Mr. Dorit, pretend your night depends on you explaining."

"Oh, good. I'm in trouble already. I got that over with early. The other fellas say the sex drops off over time. That's all."

"You spend a lot of time talking about other people's sex lives. You talk about me like that?"

"It's not like that, Eve. It's 1928. Women have been voting for almost a decade, driving cars, and cutting their hair short. The rules have changed."

She crossed her arms hiding her chest again. "Disrespect is the new rule?"

Dan sighed and picked up the cards. "Eve, please, it's our wedding night. We are in a grand hotel on the lake on your father's dime. We have pricey room service coming. Let's not fight. Show me how to play Hills and Valleys."

"You're just trying to change the subject."

"Once we are done with room service, I'm going to change the subject on you all night. If you want to play cards, you better teach me to play now, Evelyn Conroy Dorit."

Eve covered her mouth and laughed. "Evelyn Mary Dorit... Conroy sounds like a boy's middle name."

"Your robber baron daddy is not going to like that, Eve."

"Don't call him that... and I don't care what he likes. Mary is his mother's name that died when he was a boy. He'll want me to keep that."

Dan shuffled the cards once. "My guess is that he would want Evelyn Mary Conroy Dorit... or maybe me to change my name to Conroy. It is 1928."

Eve shook her head. "My father likes you fine. Don't be like that."

"He sent you two dozen roses to let you know he loves you best."

Eve shook her head. "The only way my father knew to show his disapproval of our marriage was to send flowers? Oh, yes, I see the rage now. I hope to see your disapproval regularly, Mr. Dorit."

"Ah, there is the trick, Eve. He wants to bankrupt me by giving you a taste for fine flowers."

"He is an evil genius, it seems."

"Hills and Valleys... this is a collapsing offer, as your father would say."

Eve crossed her arms again, but was smiling. Dan looked her up and down again as he shuffled against the soft spread on the bed.

"So, I'm expected to step up my wifely duties beyond what your other married, tramp friends get, but we have to hurry to play one game of cards. I see how this will be."

Dan laughed. "I will play cards with you for years... we'll play the same game continuously."

"It only goes first one to five-hundred. There are up to fifty-two points in a round, but they usually split between the players."

"We're playing to a thousand, then."

Eve fanned herself. "Oh, Mr. Dorit, please, you are giving me the vapors."

"Fine. We will play to one million."

Eve laughed. "You really won't be getting much wifely duties, if we do that."

"Oh, we'll take breaks for eating, sleeping, and such."

"And such?" Eve waved her finger at her husband.

"I'm serious," Dan said. "I'll play cards with you every night and we won't stop keeping score until one million. We are not allowed to part on to the great by and by until one player reaches the winning score of... one million points."

Eve stared at Dan. Her smile wavered, but only for a moment. Dan would see that waver on her lips in his dreams once he was in prison.

She suggested. "If we are in fact staving off death with this promise, then I say we set the bar at a billion."

"Oh, Dear Eve, I see your one billion and raise you to an even trillion."

He shuffled the cards one last time to punctuate his statement.

Eve shrugged. "Are you sure about that promise, Dear Dan? No one wants to live forever."

"Not forever," Dan set the deck on the bed between them. "Just to one trillion points... fifty-two at a time, I understand."

"Consider it our final vow of our wedding then."

Eve extended her hand. Dan shook it and then kissed her knuckles.

"Why did you invent your own game instead of just playing hearts, spades, or gin?"

Eve dealt out the cards. "My parents didn't think cards were appropriate for ladies. We weren't allowed to learn other games, so we snuck a deck and made up our own."

"Teach me the rules before you run me up on points and I never catch up."

Eve spread the cards out face up on the bed. "Tens, eights, and sixes are hills and connect trails of points. Other number cards are valleys. Face cards are bridges that steal or reassign points and create forks in the trails. Jacks and Aces are collapsing cards that break bridges. Suits or numbers can be used to connect cards in a trail. Once all cards that can be played are played, the opponent gets a point for each card left in the other's hand and then the points are assigned to each player according to the hills and bridges played."

Dan nodded. "I'm ready. I will destroy you at this game."

Eve snorted and covered her mouth and nose with her hand. "That's the spirit, Dear Dan. Once your dreams are dashed, you can always hope for room service to save you."

"I'm hoping for room service, but for different reasons. You'll be needing someone to save you."

Eve pulled a notepad and a fountain pen from the table behind her next to the silver vase and her flowers. She drew a cross on the paper. Above one arm, she wrote a "D." Above the other, she wrote an "E."

"Just shuffle and redeal, Mr. Dorit."

★

She wrapped her arms around his neck and he winced. She held on anyway and kissed him full on the mouth. He was still wincing when she drew away.

"Is it that painful to see me again, Mr. Dorit?"

"Let's get away from this dock, Eve. All this screaming and chaos is making my head hurt."

They began walking. Other soldiers and sailors embraced wives and strangers for kisses. Streamers and confetti were flying around and off the ship like a parade.

Eve took Dan's hand. "They are just glad to have everyone home. They are glad to be home. I'm glad you are home."

"Not everyone is home."

Eve leaned on his shoulder. "All the more reason to be thankful. Thank God this war is over in Germany and Japan. I was afraid they were going to send you to the Pacific, but the killing is over."

"I had plenty of points… after the injuries. The killing is never over. It slows down… but someone is always being killed. Just not me."

They reached the head of the dock and stopped. The street was more full than the offloading area.

"Where are your bags, Dan? Your trunk?"

"I didn't bring anything. I don't want anything from this… awful… Where did people get all this damned cut paper. Isn't there rationing?"

"Not anymore… the car is this way."

Dan just stood and stared at the ground with the blare of noise around him. There was a trumpet or a bugle playing in the distance. He closed his eyes.

"Do you want something to eat? We could celebrate four missed birthdays… for both of us. We can get thirty-seven candles and share a cake. We could skip eating and just get… room service. I'll let you change the subject to anything you like, Dear Dan. What's your pleasure?"

Dan kept his eyes closed as Eve held his hand in both of hers. "I want to play cards."

"Really? You are back from war and you want to play cards?"

"Do you remember the score?"

"Of Hills and Valleys? Yes, it is 48,527 to 49,473… just where we left it when you shipped out in forty-two. I looked at the notepad at least once a week."

"That's a long way from a trillion."

Eve stood beside him silently for a long moment. The bugle blurted off tune again. Dan winced. Eve pulled on his arm until he started walking with her toward the car. He kept his eyes closed the entire time she drove him home.

✱

"Deal the cards again."

Eve's hands shook. She tried to blink back the tears, but they fell thick on their flowered tablecloth. Her lips wavered into a grimace that looked like a smile. Her hands shook as she dealt the cards. The grimace quivered and then vanished.

"This one is winner take all… one trillion points for the winning hand."

Eve's nose was clogged as she sniffed and then whispered, "Why, Dan?"

"Just play."

They worked their way through two drops. Dan had to draw on his third turn. Eve's cards fell out of her hand on the table as she tried to play one.

Dan raised the barrel of the gun above the hill she had played on her last turn. "Pick up you cards, Eve."

She began crying and tried to cover her face.

"Pick up your damn cards before I ruin your face and watch it heal slowly where you lie on the floor. Pick them up!"

Eve raked the cards up from the table. She shook as she tried not to spill them again. "I don't understand… Dan?"

"Take your turn, woman."

He did not lower the weapon as he played one-handed.

Dan won on the final card. He stared up at her shaking with her last four cards in her hand. He didn't bother counting. He took the pen and used the point to turn the notebook around so the current cross was upside right for him. He drew one line through his score of 48,548. He wrote out in capital letters: ONE TRILLION.

Dan dropped the pen and smiled. Eve held her four cards and stared at the gun. He turned it away from her and placed the bore against his temple. He was still smiling.

"Dan, don't... whatever this is... shell-shock... just don't. Don't do this. Don't leave me again. Don't hurt yourself. Please, don't. Please!"

"Dear Eve, shut up. Don't make the last sound I hear in this world... a crying woman."

He looked down at the paper again and stopped smiling. The gun barrel slid down his cheek and came to rest on the table in his limp hand.

Eve dropped her four cards and reached out for the gun on the table. "Thank God, Dan."

He tightened his grip and lifted it, aiming at her face again.

✳

Dan was sitting on the porch when the police arrived. They had him stand by their car with one patrolman as they went inside. When they came back out, they had the patrolman cuff him and put him into the back of the car. They called for more officers.

Dan licked his lips. Some of the salty splatter on his face got in his mouth. He tried to spit it out twice.

"You spit in this car and I'll crack your skull open."

He licked his lips again and swallowed.

As it got dark, they drove him toward the police station.

"Why did you do it, Dorit? You rattled from the war?"

"The paper faded?"

"What?"

"The score... it vanished right off the page as I was staring at it. We can't cheat. I should have died over there, but... that cursed game knit me back together one... one painful piece at a time. There's no cheating the vow, you see."

"Save the crazy talk for your lawyer, Dorit. The Conroys are going to have you buried in pieces."

✳

Dorit stared down at his arm in the infirmary bed. He laughed loudly until one of the other prisoners jerked against his restraints in a bed down the ward and cursed Dan into silence.

"So, shut up or I'll shut you up once we're back in the block."

Dan rolled over into his pillow as far as the leather straps holding him to the bed rails would allow. "It took me until 1958 to figure this out. I'll take myself out in pieces."

He flexed his right forearm. The restraint held to the wrist with the bandage over the stump where his hand should have been. It wasn't healing back. The flesh wasn't reattaching the dead limb like on the French beach after the explosion. A new hand wasn't sprouting in its place like some species of lizard or plant.

"I've found the secret... cut away a piece at a time until there is nothing left."

"Shut up, Dorit... I'll make you suffer, if you don't."

"I wish you would... hell, I'll do it for you."

"Just shut up, man."

Dan grunted as he pulled against the leather cuff with his wounded arm. His shoulder joint began to ache. The amputation of his hand wasn't completely healed. He was feeling wetness and pain under the bandage. As his wrist pulled loose from the loop in the strap, the bandage pulled off, revealing the raw stump.

Dan hissed and pressed the arm against his chest as he waited for the throbbing to stop.

He took two, slow breaths and then leaned over to his other wrist and intact hand.

"For now..."

With the extra slack, he was able to close his teeth on the belt for the strap pulling it away from the connecting loops.

He muttered. "Won't they be surprised when they find me?"

✴

Dan was brought into the visiting room for the first time since his lawyer met with him and quit after his second failed suicide in fifty-eight. He had no family or friends inside or outside the prison. Evelyn's sister had died since his arrest and the next generation of Conroys were not interested in pursuing visits or death penalties for their aunt's killer.

The guards pushed him down into the chair and shackled him to the table through the holes on the top. They pulled at both of his hands to be sure they were locked. As they left him alone in the room, he rolled his ten fingers to try to get the circulation going.

The door on the opposite end of the room opened and Dan's mystery visitor entered. She sat down at the other end of the table. He closed his eyes.

"Dear Dan, you can't even gaze upon your lovely bride? I swallowed my teeth and the bullet on your third shot. They grew right back and my stomach wasn't right for a week."

He opened his eyes again. "Why are you here?"

"It's visiting hours, Mr. Dorit."

"I'm not permitted visitors since my last murder in fifty-eight."

"Who did you murder, Dan?"

"Myself... almost. They found me unconscious after I cut out my own brain. I had grown everything back. I was unconscious and naked in my own blood in the floor of the infirmary surrounded by body parts they assumed to belong to a second murder victim they have yet to identify. I've been in solitary ever since."

"What did you tell them about your hand magically growing back?"

"You've been following my work, Eve. They assumed I had faked the injury to get at someone in the infirmary."

"What did they say about the body parts when no one was missing?"

"I just told them I didn't catch the fella's name, but he had it coming."

Eve actually laughed. "Very funny."

"I've been paying for that joke for years."

Her smile wavered and she looked away as it dropped back into a frown. Dan shivered and had to look away from her mouth too.

"It's almost my birthday again. We've missed several more since you got back from the war."

"What is the date?"

Eve looked hurt. "My birthday is April fifteenth... tax day... remember?"

"I mean, what year?"

Eve's features softened. He still remembered them being torn away by bullets splattering their flowered tablecloth.

"It's 1963."

"Did I miss anything important?"

"A few things, Dear Dan."

"Why are you here? How?"

"I healed, just like you did."

Dan shook his head. "No, I get that. How did you get a visit when I'm in here for your murder?"

Eve tilted her head. "I'm going by Mary Daniels. Before that, I was Alice Wake. People notice when women don't age. I'm playing a journalist in this life. I used some stashed Conroy money to grease the wheels for exclusive interviews."

"Interviews... plural? What do you want to ask, Mary Daniels?"

"How do they not notice that you look young for a man closing in on sixty?"

Dan rubbed his fingers together and stared at the table. "I spend a lot of time in the dark... most of them don't care. We'll see in another twenty years or so."

Eve slid the notepad across the table. It stopped against one of his shackle chains. He tried to back away, but his hands locked the chains out tight against the underside of the table. The page was yellowed and was flecked with a splatter of brown, dried blood. The score read 48,548 to 49,518. Eve had the strong advantage.

"I went back in after I woke up naked in the coroner's office. The police left it right there on the table. I wrote in the real score from our last hand before I slipped away for good. I have some of our old photo albums, if you want me to bring next time."

"No... next time?"

"We're going to play cards once a week. I'm a little wary of living forever, so we are going to play an hour a week until we get to one trillion... fair and square."

"One hour a week isn't enough... we'll be here... years... more than years. We have to figure out something else."

She stood up and pulled out a rose from her coat. She held it up for Dan to see. He shivered, but didn't look away. Eve laid it gently down on her end of the table.

"I used to feel rage. I watched my families' funerals from a distance. Then... I understand the confusion and pain you felt healing up from the unhealable wounds, but... I'm disappointed you didn't handle it better. You didn't handle it with me. We are in this... situation together and we can only get out together. I'll see you next week."

She ran her fingertips over the petals and pulled one away. She walked toward the door. Dan slid the notepad back across the table. It stopped shy of the rose she had left him. She looked over her shoulder at it and then back at Dan.

"You need to grow up, Dan. You are almost sixty. We will be using that notepad a while... and several more after it."

"I'm not allowed to keep anything. The guards would take it, Eve... Dear Eve... we don't want to have to start over."

✱

She gave up on the shovel and pitched it over the collapsing dirt beside her. She took the hammer to the pine that was still fresh with the dirt scraped away. She broke through the boards finally and pulled away shards and splinters with the claw.

The lid collapsed under her feet and she cut her ankles trying to step back off the body inside. She used the claw of the hammer to pull herself back over the heap onto the grass. Dirt spilled through the shattered lid onto the crotch and legs.

She lifted the wine bottle to her mouth and swallowed the last swig. She pitched it away and hissed from the stinging blisters on her palms.

"You would heal faster if I cut you clean off... ridiculous."

She picked up the canteen and took another drink. The dirt around her mouth turned to mud and she wiped it away with her sleeve.

Eve stepped to the edge of the open grave and poured the rest of the canteen onto the face of the body. It splattered for several seconds before the eyes popped open and Dan began choking. She continued to pour. He rolled to his side gagging. She dropped the empty canteen in the dirt. He still looked dead.

"Climb out yourself... make it quick. We need to be on the road before daybreak."

Dan fell back in as the dirt collapsed. He coughed and clawed his way further up to the level ground in the midst of the nameless graves.

"Move, Dan... they are going to think I slipped you the razor you used to off yourself."

"You did slip it to me. They probably don't care much." Dan rolled to his back next to his grave.

"God, you are stupid sometimes, Dan. What took you so long? Were you scared?"

"I had to swallow it. It cut its way through my insides for two days before it came back out."

"I hope it hurt."

Dan rolled up to his knees and stood with some effort. "Do you want to drive? It is 1971. The rules have changed, I hear."

He looked at her just as the blade of the shovel crashed into his temple on the exact spot where he once held the barrel of the gun he used to shoot his wife. He toppled to the ground and his arms folded into his chest as his muscles spasmed. He watched her drive the blade into the ground next to him as she sat on the ground and watched.

"You had it coming... now hurry up and die already... we need to get going soon."

Dan closed his eyes as his arms went limp.

✶

Dust fell from the block ceiling onto the table. Dan started to brush it away, but stopped when the cards started to shift. Dan had to draw once he checked the ends of all the trails again. There were voices outside, but the words weren't clear. They both paused to stare at the cinderblock beside them. The noise receded. Eve played her next card. Dan had to draw again.

"Who could that be?"

"I don't know, but they'll regret surfacing soon enough."

Eve looked around the trails again carefully. Dan scratched at a sore on the back of his hand as he waited. The flesh around the wound was blackened and crisp.

"It won't heal if you keep picking at it, Dear Dan." Eve played a bridge taking most of Dan's points.

Dan drew the last card from the stack. "Is that a joke?"

Eve dropped her last card and began pointing the piece of chalk as she counted points. Dan laid out his remaining cards for her. She scratched at the board and erased the old score with her discolored finger.

"Not a joke really... a habit, I guess."

"Should we try to walk out of the radiation zone?"

"It is pretty far... I say we wait it out for now. It is our anniversary by the way."

Dan gathered the cards slowly into a stack blowing the dust off each one. "Stores were closed... I couldn't get you anything."

"Yeah, that's why."

"Remind me what year it is again."

"You don't want to know."

"What's the score?"

"You don't want to know. Just shuffle."

"Humor me."

"It is 35,645,407 to 35,656,558… and 2136."

Dan spilled the cards on his first attempt. He reached down and gathered a couple that fell onto the bunker floor.

"You're leading?"

"Always."

Dan gathered the deck into two stacks and bent them back slowly. They rattled together. He pushed them together into one deck. He closed his eyes and breathed deeply before he separated them again. Eve didn't offer to help.

✳

Dan finished shuffling and dealt again. He sorted his cards in his hand. A piece of the bark crumbled away from the two of hearts. "We'll need to cut a new deck soon."

"We could repaint them."

"They are crumbling."

"Just fix the ones breaking… save time."

Eve played the first card. Dan shook his head and drew a card.

"We'll need to stop for food soon."

"I'll go later."

"I'm hungry now."

"You go get food then, Dear Eve."

She played her next card. They went through several rounds in silence.

Dan dropped his last card and laughed. "I actually won one."

"We should get some roses to celebrate."

Dan gathered the cards while Eve scratched the points into the next blank spot on the cave wall under the cross carved into the stone. He tried to wrap his brain around the word. He started to ask, but then remembered what she meant.

"Yeah… they don't exist anymore. I could probably find a related species. I think they are poisonous now though."

"Just the food then."

"What's the score?"

Eve tracked across her columns of code. "425,848,334,705 to... 425,848,545,989... I'm still winning, but you're catching up."

Dan picked up a spear and walked toward the mouth of the cave. "This would go faster, if you would just run away with it."

"We can't cheat... we've tried, haven't we?"

Dan left the cave and made his way down the mountain slope. He tried to remember the name of the range back when humans ruled the Earth. The name escaped him. He followed the edge of the savannah around the curve of the range.

He looked back to the west where the sun was dropping away. He thought about walking. He would just walk toward the sun and leave Eve behind. It would disappear and rise again behind him. He would keep going until he reached it. He had nothing but time. He would keep going until he reached it and let its heat consume him. As he looked across the flat plain and the growing shadows, he felt like he was forgetting something. There was some trick to the world that made it harder to reach the sun, but he couldn't recall it now. He would just keep walking until he got to the edge of the world and was set free on the disc of the sun.

It was time. He negotiated the trail toward the break in the rock. He could hear the bats screeching as they began to wake. They were a little bigger than they used to be, but nothing to be frightened about just yet.

"Just more to eat."

He crouched below the mouth of the cave and waited. He wondered how many more times he would have to do this.

"We're not even halfway done."

ARMITAGE & ISEMBARD
(Noughts Vs. Crosses)
By Natalie Perry

Armitage looked at his little brother, Isembard. They had been abandoned in the prime of their youth by their Mother. If he didn't think of something for them to do soon, there would soon become the very serious risk for both of them of actual death by boredom.

Isembard was blissfully unaware of the risk he was in. He had never really experienced boredom, it was something his big brother Midge talked about a lot and didn't seem like much fun, so he just left it well alone. If he was aware that he and his brother were skirting death, he was doing a good job of not showing it. He blissfully lay on his front, sifting through the carpet fuzz, hunting for miniature treasures. So far he had found:

Anonymous Substance A, which was very possibly a stale biscuit crumb. Sampling Anonymous Substance A featured high on his to do list for later in the day.

Anonymous Substance B, which definitely looked like it had migrated indoors on the sole of somebody's shoe. He was particularly excited by Anonymous Substance B as, with a few whiffs, he had confirmed that it definitely may be, at least partially, made up of some kind of poo! This would need further investigation.

He had also excavated a series of small, coloured confetti stars which lay importantly in a tiny pile on the white part of a red and white box. This, along with several very interesting hairs and some fluff which may, or may not have tumbled from an unsuspecting belly button, made up the treasure of Isembard The Great's morning of exploration into the thick weave of the carpet of the place in which he and his only sibling had been abandoned.

Armitage watched his brother perform a small celebratory tummy wiggle dance on the floor as he held a tiny blue star up and inspected it as though it was priceless and then delicately placed it with all the other stupid things he had collected. The stars seemed to have been put there to torment them, a sign to indicate there had been children left here to rot previously. At least one lucky child's parents loved them enough to leave them with some sort of craft set containing shiny stars. All they had been left with was a pile of paper, a pen, not even a coloured pen! Just a boring black, boring biro, some game called Monopoly, which looked boring, and a packet of Toffos which had been all but completely devoured within seconds of their Mother leaving them.

Earlier in his efforts to entertain himself, Armitage had pulled a chair over to stand on and watch the fish in the tank set high into the wall, but their obvious boredom made his worse. He momentarily found release from the death strangle of inactivity when he thought one of the goldfish had died. There had been high hopes of the other fish ferociously striping their expired tank-mates carcass, as he had heard somewhere does happen. For a while he had shouted encouragingly at the surviving fish that they would suffer the same ill fate if they didn't nourish their tiny bodies with that of another. However, his shouting and glass tapping only seemed to startle the dead fish back into activity. Poo! He flumped back onto the floor to watch his simple brother's slow progress across the floor, systematically examining each row of the carpet weave minutely.

After having watched Iz celebrate the fifth short and curly hair he'd coaxed from the floor, Midge decided something had to be done! Deep in the icy numbness of his brain he could feel the bony fingers of death reaching towards him. This boredom would be the end of them if he didn't do something... Anything... Soon!

In desperation he lashed out, grabbing the biro pen with one hand and the sheets of paper with the other, as if they were some kind of lifeline.

"Hey, Iz." he said, with a slightly crazed twinkle in his eye. "Ever played noughts and crosses?"

"Nope!" came the distracted reply from the great carpet explorer.

"What?!! Everyone's played noughts and crosses!" It was the easiest game ever, it was a known fact that it had been used the world over for generations to relieve boredom and prevent people who had been shipwrecked and the like from eating each other.

If Iz learnt the rules, they could play and it would be entertainment! Who knows how long for, but it would give him a tiny glimpse into something beyond this nothingness and allow him to remember what it was like not to be wholly consumed by boredom.

Right! It was his job as big brother to teach his little brother this game and snatch them both from the jaws of death. Though they still had a

Toffo each, which he had wrestled off Iz and was storing in his pocket to put of the eventuality of death by starving. Those toffees wouldn't last forever and he would have to find a way of preventing his brother from nibbling on his dying body like some kind of depraved goldfish.

This was their only hope!

Isembard's attention was caught as Armitage smoothed out the paper on the floor. He was filled with the excitement that always arrived when a blank piece of paper presented itself. The possibilities! Endless possibilities of worlds to be drawn, animals to be invented, people to draw who weren't restricted by reality to a limited amount of fingers and toes and what's a neck for anyway? If only he could somehow get the pen off Midge... He could hide his carpet treasure and draw a treasure map! Complete with pirates and sea monsters! He could...

"Pay attention." demanded Armitage, rapping his easily distracted brother on the head with the pen. He drew a little grid in the centre of the blank page. He concentrated as he drew the two parallel lines across and two down. He could feel it, the potential of being actively de-bored by the task at hand; he finished feeling a little giddy with anticipation.

Iz could sense the energy coming from his brother and felt sure that something wonderful was about to come of this little criss crossed doodle. He gazed, pretending to pay attention as his brother said something about O's and X's and rows. His eye fixed on the precious and glorious pen. If he could just get hold of it the paper and all its glory would be at his mercy.

Armitage very carefully drew a little circle in the middle of his grid.

"Now you need to draw an X." He demonstrated on the top left hand corner of the page and pointed to it, "X's, only draw X's... Got it?"

"Yup, yup, yup." came the eager reply.

He handed the pen over to his brother, and almost immediately he saw that this was the wrong thing to do. A fire lit in his little brother's eyes as he snatched the pen and before Armitage's eyes the page filled with crosses, hundreds of them! A whole city of X's were being built, X people taking X dogs for a walk, criss cross cars with criss cross wheels driving down criss cross streets.

Both amazed and shocked by the scene unravelling in front of him, Armitage found himself unable to move to stop his brother, who was now onto his third sheet of paper building a park of X tree's and X birds pooping X's on unsuspecting X people and, he couldn't be sure, but he thought there might be little pieces of X litter being abandoned by this mad race of letters that occupied the far end of the alphabet.

Finally snapping out of the daze, Armitage decided he needed to take power back and regain control of the situation. He grabbed the pen and paper back from the frenzied doodle monster that was sat where his brother had been only moments ago.

In a second Isembard had been snapped from his exciting world that he had been introduced to by his wonderful older sibling, and was puzzled by the negative response that awaited him back in the real world.

"No! No, no, no!"

He had done something wrong.

"You have missed the point of the game!" The pen was jabbed at one of the clusters of crosses, "Look! You can't even see the grid anymore!"

"That's their house," Iz replied, "Where all the people live." He said the second part slowly, unable to believe that his very clever big brother didn't realise this obvious fact.

"Right!" A fresh sheet of paper was smoothed out, the battleground redrawn and the rules were once again explained. This time Midge watched his brother's face and anytime he saw the familiar glazed look attempted to make an appearance, he would rap the paper with the pen. He could almost hear the cogs grinding in his brother's tiny brain, trying to grasp the concept of the game. A small part of him appreciated the effort that was obviously going into this. Once again he drew an O in the centre of the grid and handed the pen over to Iz who took it with a look of great importance.

Isembard looked nervously at the paper and then back up to his brothers face who smiled and nodded encouragement, he poised the pen and... x,x,x,x,x,x,x,x!!! Da naaaaaaa! He had won! He jumped up, gripping the piece of paper that declared him the victor and was halfway through one of his more energetic celebratory dances when...

" You idiot!"

"What?!!!" He put his foot, that had been caught mid-stomp, down.

"Your only supposed to draw one X!"

"Oh!"

A third time. Not losing his patience, teeth gritted and overwhelmed with frustration, but patience is a virtue, so with forced and concentrated patience he gripped the pen and drew another tiny circle in the middle of another grid. Forcing a smile, he handed the pen to Iz who received it with an equally forced smile.

Looking from the pen to the paper, he took a deep preparatory inhalation and moved the pen to the top left hand corner of the grid. He looked to his brother and receiving an encouraging smile gave him the confidence to do what he had to do. Isembard dragged the pen across the grid from the top most corner, through the little O and down to the bottom right corner, he did the same the other way and looked at his lovely big X that crossed the entire grid. He nodded in satisfaction, a good job well done.

"Oh my god!" Armitage slapped a disbelieving hand to an even more disbelieving head.

"What?! One cross!" said Iz, pointing at his masterpiece with pride.

A calming breath was drawn. "You do a small cross, in one of the small squares, then I do a small circle in another and we take it in turns until one of us have 3 in a row!"

"Oh!"

"Yes!"

Iz looked at his hands and twisted the pen through them nervously.

"What's the matter?" Asked Armitage

"Well, I don't know really, but… it doesn't sound very… fun."

"How do you know? We haven't managed to get it right yet."

They started again and this time Iz drew a small X in a box and Midge breathed a deep sigh of relief. Mission Accomplished! Boredom would no longer nibble at their toes and strike them down in this time of parental abandonment.

Whilst the older brother was thinking this, little did he know that his little brother on the other hand was thinking that he was just discovering what it was to be bored and was worrying what his fun mechanism would do if it found out it was not being fulfilled.

Armitage drew a circle.

Isembard, nearly sweating with concentration, drew another little X.

Armitage parried the attack that he wasn't even sure that his brother even understood he had made. Handing the pen back to Iz, it all went wrong. Something had snapped, a mania washed over him…

Why did this always have to happen? Thought Armitage.

Though he was used to it, he didn't have time to prepare himself, in no time his small wriggly brother, all limbs and teeth was upon him! The pen gripped threateningly in his hand he managed to pin his big brother down just long enough to pen a large O on his forehead. He then turned the pen upon himself and drew a wonky X upon his own brow. Now completely confused, Armitage stopped trying to escape and peered at his brother.

It was then that Isembard started up his monologue, "I have marked the beast as my nemesis and my equal, though the fight has gone from him, I know just the method to re-awaken the inner savage."

"What are you talking about?" asked Armitage still pinned to the floor.

SMACK!

"Ouch! You slapped me?! You git! You're going to pay for that…"

The noble X Knight sprung to the defence as the O Monster charged. The O Monster seemed to be the one attempting something of a boxing attack whilst the X Knight was biting and growling much more then one would think knights are supposed to.

✱

The pen exchanged hands several times, O's and X's were administered by both of the fighting parties. When the X Knight was in a headlock and had his teeth sunk deeply into his opponents arm, there was a click at the far end of the room. A door opened and voices drifted through.

"Thank you for coming, Mrs Blinkerton, we'll have you back for your 6 monthly check up, just keep flossing."

"Thank you for seeing me, I hope your receptionist feels better soon… Boys!" Mrs Blinkerton saw her two sons standing in the middle of a ruin of a waiting room trying to look innocent. Both covered in scratches, bruises and what looked like… hundreds of noughts and crosses?

"I only left you for 20 minutes!"

THE FORFEIT

By Sandra Unerman

Viola, Dowager Lady Farrimond, quarrelled with her daughter-in-law on the way home from the Michaelmas Ball. Until they entered the carriage, Viola was in a glow of good humour. She was pleased with the trim bearing of her son Oliver and her grandson Ned, with the charm and delicacy of Kate and Anne, her granddaughters and pleased with the elegance of her own gown and the emerald tiara in her own dark hair, still scarcely touched with grey. She was sufficiently content with Charlotte, Oliver's wife, not to remind her more than once as they set off that, in former days, the Ball would have been held at Dillydown Hall, the Farrimonds' own house. Viola's husband had died five years ago, in 1878, and had been ill for some time before that. But even now, Charlotte seemed to have no ambition to take over the position in the county Viola had occupied in her heyday.

"So much worry," Charlotte had said. "We will enjoy ourselves much better at the Wilmotts'."

Viola had not argued. And when they arrived at the ball, they were greeted with flattering enthusiasm by their hosts. All had gone swimmingly until the moment when Charlotte put her hand on Viola's arm and said, "Your friends are in the card room upstairs. Would you like Ned to take you to them?"

It was hard to say what caused Viola more irritation: the assumption that she was fit for nothing at a ball but to play cards or that she needed an escort to find her way upstairs. But her skills in combat had been learned from worthier opponents than poor Charlotte. Viola smiled and turned to the handsomest man near at hand. "Later perhaps," she said. "But I see Mr Wilmott has come to claim the dance I promised him."

Young Rob Wilmott looked a touch puzzled but he was too well brought-up to give her away. He bowed and offered his arm. And if he would rather have been waltzing with Kate or Anne, he did not show it. His eyes sparkled at Viola's banter and her stories about his uncles and his tutors at Oxford. When the dance was over, she asked him to introduce her to his friends and he laughed outright. "Of course. But will you save me a dance later on. I have not had such a good partner all year."

Viola had not danced the night away for ten years or more. She was pleased to find she could still keep going, even if her ankles ached by the time the carriages were summoned. One or two of her partners had been tongue-tied and others overbold but she had enjoyed reassuring the former and quelling the latter. And she had danced twice with the man every young woman in the county adored; Sir Rowland Worth, tall, melancholy and charming.

They travelled back as they had come, Sir Oliver in one carriage with his daughters, Viola and Charlotte in the other with Ned. Viola settled into her fur wrap and prepared to drowse in the chilly air. "A very good evening," she said. "Did you enjoy yourself, Charlotte?"

"Not altogether," Charlotte answered slowly. "Ladyma, I beg your pardon but I must speak to you."

"Then I wish you would call me by my name," Viola grumbled, but mildly. "What is the matter, child?"

"I don't like to see—" Charlotte stopped and then started again. "I hate to watch the way you let those young men make fun of you. I am sorry: I don't want to hurt you but you must know, for your own sake, as well as for the sake of Oliver and the girls."

"Make fun of me?" Viola sat upright, her drowsiness flattened by fury. "How dare you think so?"

"None of the other grandmothers danced more than one dance." Charlotte's voice shook but her meaning was clear enough. "None of the married women danced with all the eligible young men under thirty. What else can anyone think?"

"Queen Elizabeth the Great danced until she was on her deathbed," Viola answered. "I never heard that she confined herself to elderly widowers for her partners. You are a fool, Charlotte."

"Those days were long ago," Charlotte said. "Ask Ned what he would have thought if Lady Wilmott's mother had asked him to dance."

Ned was fifteen, four years younger than Rob Wilmott. When Viola glanced at him she saw that he had gone green with terror and was bent forward, staring rigidly at his bootcaps. Viola said, "Ned is too tired to think straight. And so, no doubt, are you. Good night, Charlotte."

★

Fury sustained Viola throughout the rest of the drive home. She remained calm during the brief gathering with the occupants of the other carriage and the gossip before they all went to bed. She saw Oliver frown as he looked from Charlotte's face to hers but he said goodnight as usual. She had told her maid not to wait up, so it was Kate who unhooked the back of her dress and helped her off with her jewellery. Not until Kate had gone and Viola sat alone at her dressing table to brush out her hair did the tide of anger ebb away to leave her cold and miserable. In the candle-light the white threads hardly showed: her hair looked as bountiful and splendid as when she was Kate's age. And she could remember the long-ings that had filled her then, not just to become a wife and mother like any other girl but to find out a destiny all her own, to become learned, to have adventures, to become a famous singer or the muse of a great man. Then she had met Gilbert Farrimond, as moody and passionate as she was herself. After a bout of fascinating quarrels, she had married him and exercised her talents as his wife, the chatelaine of the household and the centre of the world they both occupied in London and here in the coun-try. Now he was dead and Charlotte was the centre of the world. But Viola was not yet ready to dwindle into grandmotherhood. She brushed her hair with fierce strokes until her eyes watered and her hands shook.

✷

In the soft afternoon light, the stone steps of the Twisty Bridge loomed grey and smooth among the willow branches. Viola stopped to catch her breath before she began to climb up. She had tried to outwalk the ill-humour still acute when she woke this morning and partly succeeded. Her errands in the village had gone well, the red berries on the thorn bushes and the yellow leaves in the stream pleased her eye. But she was in no hurry to return to the Hall, especially as she would be asked questions about her solitary day. She turned to look back down the hill and did not notice the stranger until he spoke.

"Come up onto the bridge. The view is better and the wind is not cold today."

She turned and saw him at the top of the steps, a man with legs so long he might have been able to step across the stream without troubling the bridge. His shoulders were wide and his arms long but he was thin, more like a scarecrow than a giant. He wore a rust-coloured coat lined with black and a round, red hat, which he took off with a bow, as Viola gazed at him.

"Good afternoon," she said. He did not belong to the village and she had heard of no such visitor round about. But he did not look like a tramp. This path was not a right of way and Folly Bridge, as it was called on the map, led nowhere much except the Hall. But the Farrimonds never minded harmless ramblers. Besides, Viola's curiosity was a welcome change from her preoccupations. She climbed the steps. "Have you come far?"

He grinned. "You might think so. Sit down, Lady Farrimond, and rest while we talk."

There was a bench cut into the wall over the crown of the bridge. Viola had meant to sit there to enjoy the tangle of colours in the hawthorn bushes and the deepening blue of the sky. She stood still and considered the stranger. No doubt he had guessed who she was from talk in the village.

"You have the advantage of me?"

He took a step back and leaned against the opposite wall. "Call me Thornling and ask what you want to know. If you make guesses, you will disappoint us both."

"Indeed!" Viola took the shawl from round her shoulders and folded it into a cushion to sit upon. "Who are you, young man, and what are you doing here?"

He grinned again, to her irritation. But he said, "I am a scholar and a wanderer. I go where my studies take me."

"And what aspect of your studies brings you here?"

"That depends," he said and fell silent, watching Viola. Her irritation faded, lost in fascination and maybe a touch of fear. She had called him young: his pale skin was delicate and he moved with the suppleness of a child. But his hair was grizzled and his glance matched hers in sharpness and authority. He made her think of the heroes of her childhood, Sir Walter Raleigh and Lord Byron, and how she had once meant to be an explorer, not of lands overseas but into the dark woods and ancient remains of her home.

She could not tell whether they sat in silence for two minutes or two hours before Thornling put his hand into the pocket of his coat and drew out a pack of cards. "Do you play ecarté, my lady?"

Despite her rebellion at the ball, Viola was a keen card player. But she had never played before against a chance acquaintance in the middle of nowhere. As she hesitated, Thornling slid the cards from their pack and began to shuffle them. The design was not one Viola recognised. The cards were large and their backs patterned with swirls of red, gold and brown. She wanted a closer look.

"I have time for one game," she said. "Then I must go home before the family miss me."

The cards were hand-painted and made of heavy parchment. The backs were covered with a pattern of twisted tree branches, or maybe they were roots, through which scattered human faces looked out, interspersed with fox heads, badgers and hedgehogs. The four suites were oak and ivy leaves, toadstools and spiders; the court cards animals dressed in robes of state. Viola could not guess where they had been made.

"Tell me of your travels," she said.

"I have come from a feast with the night wolves of the north. They find it easier to enter men's dreams now so many lie close together in the great cities but the food they find within is meagre fare. What do you dream about, Lady Farrimond?"

"Nothing that belongs in a fairy tale," Viola felt the cold suddenly, settling round her clothes and creeping over her skin. She looked up: the sun was still well above the horizon and the sky was cloudless, promising a cold night. She had never heard of night wolves and would have asked for more description, if one of her grandchildren had told her a tale about them. But not here. She was tempted to throw the cards down and hurry home but then she would despise herself later.

Viola won the game. Thornling smiled at her as he gathered up the cards. "Well played. What forfeit will you choose?"

Viola frowned. "We didn't play for forfeits."

Thornling shrugged. "It's a poor game with nothing at stake. Choose a gift from me, as trifling as you please."

Viola looked at the cards in his hands, strange and colourful. She wanted a chance to study the patterns more carefully and to store the bright pictures in her memory. "Will you give me your pack of cards?"

Thornling's fingers crooked inwards. "I've had these a long time."

"They are beautiful," Viola said.

"So they are. But they may store more memories than you would find comfortable, of the creatures who made them and those who have played with them. Choose something else, a brooch for your shawl, perhaps, or silver buckles for your shoes."

"I would rather have the cards," Viola said. Thornling tidied the deck and handed them to her but he said:

"Will you give me chance to win them back?"

Viola lost the second game. By the end she was stiff and cold from sitting for so long. The sun had not yet set but she felt that the world might have revolved round her many times while she was preoccupied with the game and with her opponent, with the gleam of his eyes and the twist of his voice. And yet she knew little more about him than when they began. A great disappointment filled her at the loss of her winnings.

Thornling said, "Third time pays for all. Shall we play one last game?" and she nodded before she could stop herself.

The play was fiercer this time and both players moved faster. The twilight deepened round them so that Viola could hardly make out Thornling's face. But she saw the flash if his smile as he won again. He said, "Now it is your turn to pay a forfeit."

Viola's blood curdled in her head and her stomach. Had she been beguiled by a confidence trickster or something worse, further outside her experience? Whatever Thornling was, the trap was easy to see now and she would have mocked anyone else who had not the wit to draw back in time.

"What do you want?" she asked, her voice careful and slow.

Thornling laughed. "I will give you a chance to decide. What treasure of your own will you offer me, the equal of my best cards?"

Viola's mind refused to work. She said, "I have no such treasures: nothing like that."

"You have a fine house. You have lived a full life. You must have gathered some things you cherish," Thornling said and when she did not speak, he added, "I will allow you a week to decide. Come to me here a week from today and bring me a forfeit. Or I will choose one of my own."

"What do you mean?" Viola tried to sound angry instead of afraid. But Thornling laughed and when she stood up to protest, she found she was alone. She could not tell which way he had gone.

✴

The open windows of Viola's bedroom swung to and fro and the rain dripped onto the window seat. The wind shook the chandelier and sent shadows twisting over the heap of broken vases, photographs pulled from frames, smashed glass, clothes torn and trampled, spilled powder, dented combs and stained cushions. In the middle, Viola sat on the floor and croaked, "Help me! Come quickly!" She did not think anyone could hear her.

When she had started the mischief an hour ago, she had been surprised at how much she enjoyed herself. To dash her best porcelain against the iron bedposts, to drag out her clothes and stand on the hems until they ripped, to break the string of pearls her husband had given her when they were betrothed; if anyone else had done these things she would have been outraged. She felt anger now but also a kind of savage lightness, as though the destruction could set her free from her past to start her life over again. But she was exhausted by what she had done and hoarse from shouting. And the gusts of cold air made her shiver.

She leaned her head back against the side of her bed and shut her eyes to rest for a moment, before deciding what to do next. Then she dozed.

✱

"Grandmama! Grandmama, wake up!" Kate's voice was frightened.

"Not you," Viola whispered, before she remembered why she had not wanted the children to find her. "Fetch Ellen."

"Let me help you first. Can you stand up?"

Viola was stiff and her skin ached as if she had been beaten. She winced even at Kate's tentative clasp. "Where is Ellen? Why hasn't she come?"

"I'll find her." Kate stood up. "But you're so cold." She took the shawl from her own shoulders and tucked it gently round Viola before she hurried away.

✱

"Mother! What the devil has happened?"

By the time she heard her son's voice, Viola felt seriously unwell, cold and feverish as well as guilty. When she had determined on this plan, she had not realised how frightened she would make them all. But she could not stop now. "Send for the police," she said. "Maybe it is not too late to catch him."

"My lady, oh my lady." There was Ellen, who would have been much more use at the start, as a witness and to keep the others away. Viola refused to be distracted by her now but kept her eyes on Oliver, who looked astonished as well as appalled.

"Catch who?"

"The thief. I tried to stop him but he got out of the window, and the emeralds with him. Tell the police he wore a mask but I can describe his clothes."

"A thief did this?" Now Oliver looked angry. "Did he hurt you?"

"The emeralds?" Kate had come back into the room with her father. "The Farrimond tiara?"

"Nonsense," Oliver said. "The tiara is in the safe downstairs." He crouched down. "I want to get you into bed, mother."

Viola said, "I brought the tiara up here this morning. I thought one of the stones might be loose."

Oliver sat back on his heels. "You did what? Why?" He stopped and a frown bit down over his face. "Let me carry you into bed. Never mind anything else for now."

★

The next afternoon, Viola sat in bed, considerably better in body and rather worse in mind. She found the guest bedroom, redecorated some months ago to Charlotte's taste, overfrilled and overpolished but not unpleasant. The grounds of the Hall had been searched for the emeralds and people had come to hear her story, every member of the family except Charlotte. Their concern for her made Viola uncomfortable, as did the settled frown on Oliver's face, along with the questions he had not asked. She knew from Ellen that he had examined the servants, not harshly but sternly. Viola had not meant the servants to be under suspicion. She had given a long, if confused, description of the stranger she had surprised in her room.

Now Kate sat beside her bed, looking wretched. "Mamma said to leave you alone. But someone has to tell you how upset she is."

"Charlotte is upset?" This was unexpected. "Charlotte does not care about the emeralds: they are a Farrimond heirloom."

"It's not that." Kate looked more and more unhappy. "She's afraid you have hidden it because you do not want any of us to wear it."

Viola's head throbbed. Kate was a clever girl and a kind one, loyal both to her parents and her grandmother. She must feel that desperate measures were required, to come here like this. All the same, Viola said, "That would be petty and childish."

Kate nodded, biting her lip. "But no one has reported a stranger lingering in the neighbourhood. Father said no common thief would break into the Hall in the middle of the evening, while we are in residence."

"And you think I have hidden the tiara away out of jealousy?"

Kate shook her head. "But I thought of a worse reason."

"And what is that?"

Kate bent her head until Viola could not see her face and twisted her hands together. She whispered, "If one of us took the emeralds and you found out; if Ned took them…"

"Why would Ned…" Viola stopped, horrified at the suspicions she had set loose. "But there was a stranger," she said. "I played cards with him on Folly Bridge."

Kate looked up, hopeful but puzzled. "Did you bring him here?"

Viola reached for the glass of barley water beside her bed and moistened her lips. At least if she told the truth she need no longer feel ashamed, even if nobody believed her. "I'll tell you what happened," she said.

Kate listened, wide-eyed. At the end she said, "What was he like, the Thornling?"

Viola's throat hurt. She sipped barley water as she tried to find a way to explain. "Like a child who has grown up over a thousand years without growing out of childhood. Or a tree turned into a man who will turn back one day but not yet."

"What did he want?"

"He said he was a student. Maybe he studies old women with too little to occupy them?" Viola clenched her hands round her glass and tried to steady her breathing. "Do I sound ridiculous?"

"Oh no! I wish I could have an adventure like that. But I don't understand about the emeralds?"

"Your father is a good son but a stubborn man," Viola said stiffly. "If I told him that I mean to give them away, he would think I am delirious and stop me going back. Or he would try to run Thornling off the land as a vagrant. And that would bring worse trouble upon us."

"We could try to explain," Kate sounded doubtful. "But I meant, are they the right thing to choose?"

Viola said, "Those cards were hand painted and old, like a book of illuminated manuscripts. I possess nothing to match them but the emeralds at least have a history. They were worn by my husband's aunt at the ball before the Battle of Waterloo. And the tiara is beautiful."

"But it is from the wrong side of the family: a Farrimond heirloom. You said the forfeit is one of your belongings."

"One of my treasures," Viola snapped. "That's you and your brother and sister. And I will not give you up."

"There must be something else. Something that truly belongs to you."

Viola looked carefully at Kate. If she did not look, it was easy to think of her as another self, as the high-spirited young woman Viola still felt herself to be, in her deepest heart. Kate had put her hair up today but still she looked younger than her eighteen years, with her round cheeks and soft mouth. She had the pointed Farrimond chin and Charlotte's rich brown hair but she was more than the mixture of her family inheritance and had been from the moment she was born. And maybe that meant Viola's worst fears were groundless. "What would you choose?"

"I think it has to be your choice." Kate leaned forward and carefully kissed her grandmother's cheek. "You'll find the right thing. I know you will."

★

By candlelight Oliver and Charlotte sat on either side of the bed, their faces stiff and anxious. Viola looked from one to the other and straightened her back. She picked up the silk handkerchief from her lap and tipped the emeralds in front of Charlotte.

"I made a mistake," Viola looked from Charlotte to Oliver and spoke briskly. "I thought I needed them to protect the family but I have changed my mind."

"Needed them for what, Mother?" Oliver tried hard not to shout. "What has happened to you? What happened to your room?"

Viola frowned at him. "What did Kate tell you?"

Charlotte answered. "Only that you wanted to speak to us. But we don't want to weary you tonight. It will be a relief to put these under lock and key again but would you rather tell us the rest in the morning?"

"The rest doesn't matter," Viola said in her most quelling voice. "I'm sorry I frightened Kate and turned the house upside down. But the reasons are my own affair: you are better off not knowing any more."

"You frightened me as well," Oliver pointed out. "And Ellen. It may be churlish but I would like an explanation as well as an apology."

"Don't bully me, Oliver." Viola began to feel better. She watched as Oliver pushed himself to his feet and strode to the window. Charlotte said vehemently, "I hate squabbling," and they both turned to look at her. Reluctantly Viola said:

"None of this is your fault, Charlotte."

"Then what is it about?" Oliver came to stand behind his wife and rub her shoulders. "Have you been feverish?"

"Certainly not. Send for your doctor friend, if you like, and let him examine me."

Oliver eyed his mother thoughtfully, as though considering his next line of questioning. But Charlotte said, "No more tonight. Surely we will all feel better in the morning."

★

Much later, after the household had settled down for the night, Viola climbed from her bed. She lit the lamp on the unfamiliar dressing table and sat for a long time, staring at her face in the mirror. She thought about Charlotte, who would rather smooth over a quarrel than satisfy her curiosity and who could run her house and family so comfortably if Viola would leave her alone. And she thought about Kate, young and eager for adventures. But maybe Viola was the one who needed to leave home, to go to London and find a new occupation, no matter how hard that might be, away from everyone who knew her.

These thoughts brought Viola no nearer her goal, which was to find a treasure she could truly call her own, worthy of comparison with Thornling's cards. She looked at the heap of pearls from her broken necklace. They were well-shaped and of a good, translucent colour, but small, bought when Gilbert had been unable to afford anything grander. She thought of the other gifts he had given her over the years, mostly books and paintings, the furniture they had chosen together, well crafted and comely but nothing she treasured in the way she coveted those cards. She frowned into the mirror and took down her hair to brush it while she thought, as she had done when she was a girl to lull her mind and calm her spirit, as Gilbert had done for her throughout their marriage. And she stared again at the heavy fall, still soft and lively, uncut since she was seven.

★

Autumn had dropped into winter during the seven days since Viola's meeting with Thornling. Many tree branches were bare and the sun was lower in the sky. As Viola walked up to the Twisty Bridge, this time from the Hall side, she felt a damp cold clinging to her skin. Her ears and the nape of her neck were tender and newly sensitive to the touch of the air, despite the snug fit of her hat. She walked briskly and refused to think about what might happen if she had chosen wrong.

Thornling was waiting for her, even taller than she remembered, a gaunt, bony figure with eyes as keen as knife-points. He bowed and handed her up the steps onto the bridge.

"Now, my lady, what have you brought me?"

Viola took her finest silk scarf from inside her muff and unfolded it. Inside, the plait of her hair lay dark and shining, soft as the silk, supple and strong. She had threaded the loose pearls from her necklace onto white hairs, to twist round the others and bound the ends of the plait with white silk, knotted with more pearls. Viola's hands shook as she held it out and she thought that if Thornling scorned her choice, one of them would have to die before morning. But he touched the plait with gentle fingers and said:

"You are a good loser, my lady. Better than I expected."

Viola had not intended to sit down but her knees were shaking. She folded onto the stone seat, uncertain whether to laugh or cry and said, "That is not my reputation. And I do not take it as a compliment."

"You should." Thornling grinned at her. "You'll play better in the next game if you let the last one go."

Viola shook her head. "I do not plan to play cards with strangers again."

"Then you will be safer but not necessarily wiser." Thornling took the plait and tied it round his waist. Viola's breath caught in her throat. He bowed to her again. "Thank you my lady. Good luck to you, whatever games you play." He did not wait for a response but strode off towards the woods on the further slope. Viola sat in thought until the cawing of the crows over head roused her and she realised she must hurry to be home before dark.

RIOT SEASON

By David Turnbull

10:30am – 4th August

It's the height of the Riot Season. Police Constable Max Boateng steps down from the train onto the intercity platform at New Street Station. He's eight hours ahead of the next fixture and twenty-four hours behind the arrival of the rest of the national squad. He's running on nervous energy.

Max is the man of the moment. Dressed in a designer suit, donated to him by a top flight London fashion house, he has the air of a male model about him. His handsome mixed race heritage has helped the upward trajectory of his career no end.

Passengers alighting from the other carriages nudge each other as he walks briskly past them. Usually he thrives on the attention, but today he's not in the mood. His left shoulder, dislocated when a rioter lobbed half a paving stone at him during a fixture in Liverpool, is playing him up. He slips on a pair of dark glasses and hopes no one has the gall to ask him for an autograph.

At the end of the platform a huge banner billboard declares – "Birmingham welcomes Urban Riot 2032". The banner is adorned with the brand logos of the various corporations who are the season's main sponsors.

Wincing against another spasm in his shoulder he reaches into his pocket for a little lozenge of prescription painkiller and pops it into his mouth. One of the station attendants steps up to him, hand outstretched. Max gives him a grudging handshake. Somet5hing for the poor bastard to tell his kids about when they're watching the live televised coverage of tonight's riot.

The paparazzi are congregated three deep on the concourse. The staccato flash of cameras to his left and right sets off a sharp stabbing sensation in Max's head. He can feel the start of a migraine coming on. Journalists start firing questions at him.

Glennys, his agent, who's been hovering on the sidelines near the ticket barrier, materialises at his side. Her head only comes up as far as his chest. Her red hair is tied up in a severe bun. The shoulder pads on her jacket are almost as broad as those on the body armour Max will don for tonight's riot. Her make up, applied as if it is some sort of symbolic war paint, gives her a ferocious look that compliments her fearsome temperament.

"Max will only be doing pre-arranged interviews," she barks at the press, guiding him by the elbow toward the exit. "Out of the way. Out of the fucking way."

Outside a fierce yellow sun is already burning its way through the clouds. Britain has been in the grips of a relentless heat wave for three weeks now. A thunderstorm right about now would drop the temperature before the riot kicks off. Max knows from the previous midweek fixture in Newcastle that wearing a helmet, visor and full body armour in these temperatures is going to make him sweat like a pig and that's going to play merry hell with his shoulder.

Across the street a crowd of Max's loyal fans are corralled behind barriers like cattle. When he emerges onto the pavement, just behind Glennys, the two uniformed officers patrolling the front of the barrier shake their heads in affected disgust. Beat cops might claim to despise members of the national riot squad but Max suspects that most of them would secretly give their back teeth to be selected for the fixtures.

His courteous nod doesn't seem to appease them.

But, thinking the nod is for them, an ear splitting scream goes up from his fans.

It accelerates the momentum of his headache.

Max's fan base is predominantly made up of middle-aged women. They call themselves the Maxie-Mums. These ones are carrying placards depicting Max in full riot gear – the iconic image of him leading the baton charge along Glasgow's Sauchiehall Street during the '29 season – a riot fixture that sealed his reputation and moved him up into the big time.

Max waves to his fans and flashes a fake smile. His shoulder complains when he raises his arm. The pain radiates up to his head. One of the Maxie-Mums leans across the barrier and throws a pair of knickers into the road. They lie there like pink, frilly road kill.

"Stop encouraging them," hisses Glennys, bundling him into the waiting limo. Another wave of screams pulses through the crowd. From the back seat of the limo the Maxie-Mums' chant can be heard. The inane cheerleader couplet that's greeted him in every city for the past two seasons.

"Maxie, Maxie, he's the man! Who can do it? Maxie can!"

The throbbing in his head grows considerably worse. Pain stabs at his left eye. His doctor has a theory that the root cause of his reoccurring migraines is the constant flashes of light and intense noise he has to endure at the height of a riot. Apparently the condition is fast becoming commonplace amongst professional riot cops.

10:45 am

The limo sweeps through the streets of Birmingham.

Road closures are already being phased in. Decommissioned transit vans, the liveries of their previous owners still deliberately visible for product placement, are being parked up at strategic points. Beside these are cars, impounded for road tax evasion or other offences.

These vehicles are being placed at predicted flash points to tempt tonight's rioters to up their game and therefore increase the fixture's entertainment value for the punters. Max marks their positions and commits them to memory. The trick with a riot is to keep it fluid. If you allow the rioters to remain static they get the notion to dig in and erect barricades. Once they start rolling vans and cars across the roads they can seal off whole sections of a city and loot with impunity.

Bang goes your fixture bonus!

Up on the surrounding rooftops temporary spectator stands are being erected. Max clocks the location of the VIP enclosure and instinctively commits this to memory. At some point tonight he may need to play to the people who count. A mental map begins to construct itself in his head, marking spotlights installed on top of street lamps, and blast proof CCTV cameras mounted at strategic vantage points.

Know your terrain, thinks Max, up your game.

Something the squad coach always tried to drive home.

He sees his own face on several advertisements adorning the sides of passing buses. A brand of aftershave and a fast food chain are amongst those laying claim to Max Boateng's personal endorsement.

Glennys is noisily juggling bids for the post-riot interview, playing the Sunday supplements off against each another. "He's actively considering a more lucrative offer. Yes it will be an exclusive – so long as we agree on a figure. No you fucking can't have access to him in the dressing room!"

On the mini screen in the back of the limo a news reporter is interviewing a rowdy group of gang members. Max hears his name being mentioned. "Maxie Boateng, you is going down." A faceless youth affects menacing street patois from the shadowed depths of his hoodie. "You hear me, man? You is going down. Me and my boys is gunnin' for you."

He flicks two fingers over his head in a handgun gesture. Pop! Pop! Pop! His crew surge in behind him, aggressively swamping the interviewer.

Max removes his dark glasses and presses the heel of his hand against his left eye.

The phone rings.

"Add another fucking zero on the end and then call me back if you've got the balls," yells Glennys and hangs up.

Max runs his hand over his forehead.

"You got any aspirin in your handbag?"

11:05am

As they pass through the foyer of the hotel a waitress accidentally drops a coffee cup. It smashes loudly on the marble floor. The ghost image of a shop front window shattering into a billion crystal smithereens on a darkened street flashes before Max's eyes. His tinnitus kicks in – piping like a discordant penny whistle in his right ear.

He swallows down three of the aspirin from the little plastic bottle that Glennys handed to him before they emerged from the limo. Some of his fellow team members are already at the hotel bar, rowdily downing bottles of beer, despite the early hour.

"Nice of you to show your ugly face, Boateng!" goads one of them.

Max gives him the finger and slips into the lift behind Glennys.

In his hotel room Max picks up a newspaper from the pile at the foot of the bed. The headline reads "Maxie's Millions! – Is Max Boateng Avoiding Tax Through His Overseas Investments?"

"Did you know about this?" Max asks Glennys.

She is busily checking emails.

"The lawyers are onto it," she replies, not looking up from the phone. "Those bastards don't have a shred of hard evidence. But if I were you I'd get on to your accountant. Someone in that firm has a big fucking mouth."

Max switches on the TV. A couple of pundits, one male, one female, both former Riot Squad members, are discussing the upcoming fixture. "Battle hardened crews from Handsworth and Dudley are going to be out on the streets tonight," says the man. "Lads and lasses amongst them who are veterans of two or three seasons now."

"Personally I have my eyes on the crew that's travelling in from Wolverhampton," says the woman. "They're part of a growing trend for what is fast becoming known as nomads. They don't owe allegiance to any particular turf, so they're not afraid of a ruck at any fixture. This Wolverhampton lot have been seen in Leicester, Cardiff and Manchester already this season."

Glennys switches the TV off.

"I've got you a guest spot on Lunch with Loretta at midday," she says. "So you've got about half an hour for a shit, a shave and a shower before the car arrives to take you to the studio."

12:30pm

The set has been made up to look as if it is Loretta Isaac's homely front room – house plants, coffee table, Persian rug - a room divider with assorted ornaments. The presenter herself is dressed in a casual blouse and trousers combo. She is seated in a plush leather armchair, her three guests, Max amongst them, are seated side by side on a long sofa.

Max's headache isn't easing. Over the high-pitched whistling that is still persisting in his left ear he hears the tail end of the jangling Lunch with Loretta theme tune. Loretta smiles as the camera zooms in on her. Over her shoulder Max can see Glennys in the wings, tapping frantically at her phone keyboard.

"Hello and welcome to Lunch with Loretta," gushes Loretta. "Today we're coming live from Birmingham where, in just a few hours time, Urban Riot 2032 will kick off. Fitting then that the subject for discussion today is – 'Are the riots good for Britain?' My lunch guests today are Professor of Sociology from Durham University, Alice Mayhew, whose critical study of the riots – entitled 'They Predict a Riot' is currently available for download. Geoffrey Earle MP, the junior Home Office Minister widely considered to be the architect of the policy of controlled riot. And Police Constable Max Boateng of the National Riot Squad."

When Max's name is mentioned a whoop goes up from a section of the studio audience. When Max looks a dozen Maxie-Mums, all dressed in tee shirts bearing his image, have occupied an entire row of seating.

Loretta turns to the MP.

"So, Geoffrey Earle?" she asks. "Are the riots good for Britain?"

Earle leans forward and sips from a glass of water. "Well, given my involvement in their establishment I don't think you'd expect me to say anything else but yes. And the statistics bear this out. In the five years since the policy was written into statute we have seen a substantial reduction in street crime."

He starts reeling things off.

"Muggings are down by seventy-five percent, car theft is down by eighty percent, and inter-gang related incidents are down by sixty percent. The major retailers are reporting a year on year decline in shoplifting. This is all down to us being able to target police resources in a focused manner. Delinquents who may otherwise have been drawn into petty crime are, in fact, devoting themselves to training for the riots and that, in turn, is helping reduce the incidence of obesity in the young – relieving the National Health Service of a potential long-term burden."

"But, remember too, rioting and everything that goes with it is still a criminal offence – so the arrests that good men like PC Boateng make at the fixtures mean that large numbers of petty criminals are removed from inner city areas every summer."

Max finds himself zoning out as the studio lighting gnaws at his headache. His shoulder feels stiff. The whistling is relentless. He feels his eyelids start to droop. He realises he can't actually recall now how many painkillers he's swallowed in the past couple of hours.

"I would challenge those assumptions," Alice Mayhew interjects.

"They're not assumptions," says Earle. "Everything can be verified by the National Office of Statistics."

Max forces his eyes back open.

"Professor Maynard," says Loretta. "You'll have your say in a moment. But for now I want to go to our London studios where we have a former notorious rioter that I'd like to bring in. Ladies and gentlemen, with his debut single released on his own label just last week, the UK's latest rap sensation, Repeet Offenda."

Some of the younger members of the audience cheer loudly as a muscular young man with tattooed arms folded over his barrel chest appears on the screen behind Loretta.

"So, Mr Offenda," asks Loretta, "you participated in several urban riot fixtures and served six months in prison on the last occasion – in your opinion are the riots good for Britain?"

Offenda screws his eyebrows into a practiced scowl and flexes his upper arm muscles. Someone in the audience responds with a little squeal of delight that is almost sexual in its tone.

"The riots was definitely good for me, Loretta," says Offenda. "I looted 'nuff equipment to kit out my own personal recording studio. And the dosh I got back from selling bling and 'ting, I invested in my business. Now I is gone legit and my record is number one in the download chart, innit."

"And we're going to hear that very record later in the show," says Loretta.

She turns around again and faces Alice Mayhew.

"Professor," she says. "This kind of proves the point the Minister was making. Mr Offenda here has transformed himself from a street criminal to a successful recording artist and legitimate businessman to boot. From what I hear he is now providing gainful employment for several of his former gang members."

"True 'dat," nods Offenda on the screen.

Now Alice Mayhew takes a sip of water.

"From the proceeds of crime," she points out.

"That's entirely within the rules," Earle points out. "And it's partly why crime outside of the strictly controlled arena of the riots is going down."

Alice Mayhew scowls at him.

"For my book I studied a group of riot participants on a Bristol housing estate," she continues. "And the experiences of my subjects were starkly different. One of my subjects, Manjit Chowdhary, was wheelchair-bound as a result of being severely beaten by riot cops. She was then charged with criminal offences without a shred of real evidence and subsequently refused Disability Living Allowance. In fact her entire family had their benefits suspended."

"My heart bleeds," sneers Earle. "Miss Chowdhary would have known the consequences. It is mandatory that the Revised Riot Act is read out over public address systems no less than three times before the official start of a fixture."

Alice Mayhew's face flushes almost purple. "The real misfortune is that we live in a country where police brutality is openly endorsed as official government policy!"

Loretta smiles sweetly and turns to Max.

"Police brutality?" she says. "Are you a brutal man, PC Boateng?"

Max feels his head pounding.

Another stark memory flashes before him.

A darkened street – he's surrounded by at least two-dozen drug crazed teenage rioters. They close in around him, armed with iron railings and chunks of masonry. He uses his baton like a scythe to swipe the legs from under his assailants. Screaming in agony, a young girl falls to the pavement.

He can sense Loretta and the other guests waiting for his response. He sees the camera zooming in on him. He opens his mouth to speak – and then freezes.

The studio audience falls silent. In the wings Max can see the appalled look that settles on Glennys' face. She starts to mouth profanities at him. But it's like a sudden paralysis has descended on him. Painful seconds drag by before Loretta saves the day with her consummate professionalism.

"Sorry PC Boateng, I'm not going to able to take your response at the present time," she says. "I'm being told to go straight to the VT of Repeat Offenda's debut single – Lootin' on a Saturday Night."

To the sound of a menacing bass line an image of Repeat Offenda fades in on the big screen. He is bare-chested – all tattoos and oiled muscles. Behind him footage from various urban riot fixtures play out – petrol bomb volleys – upturned vehicles – baton charges. Max feels a cold sweat run down his spine. Swaggering back and forth and oozing raw belligerence Offenda begins to chant a visceral bastardisation of an old children's rhyme.

Here we go looty-loot
Here we go looty-li
Here we go looty-loot
All on a Saturday night

1:45pm

Max and Glennys are in the back of the limo again.

"Jesus fucking Christ, Max!" rants Glennys. "What the fucking, shit-ting hell was that about?"

Max shrugs and winces when his shoulder complains.

Glennys isn't even looking at him. One eye on the screen of her phone she carries on haranguing him. "What were you thinking? I get you a spot on Lunch with Loretta – Lunch with fucking Loretta, Max. The biggest daytime show ever and you just there like some deaf fucking mute!"

"I wasn't feeling too good," says Max, rubbing his eye. "I still don't, to tell you the truth."

"Get a fucking grip on yourself," Glennys snaps. "You know how much people have got riding on you."

5:35pm

Having slept all afternoon and pointedly refused to do a radio interview Glennys had arranged for him, Max is in the team dressing room beneath Birmingham's Bull Ring Centre. The rest of the squad are pumped up and raring to go. Max is only half-dressed in his kit. He's had had some physio on his shoulder but his headache hasn't eased and the tin whistle is still piping in his ear.

"Hey, Maxie," says a voice to his left. "You gonnae' gie the rest o' us a look in this time?"

PC Shona McLean is smiling down at him as she slips on her re-enforced shoulder pads. McLean only transferred to the National Squad from the Lothian and Borders Division this season but she's already snapping at Max's heels on the arrest front. She's photogenic and consciously mellows her accent for interviews. The media are starting to love her.

"You make your own chances in this game," says Max, bending down to tie his bootlace.

"Aye," says Shona. "And the first fuckin' chance I get I'm takin' it."

She turns her back and points to the straps of her shoulder pads, winking at the other team members. "Do me up would ye, Maxie?"

Max obliges, feeling himself blush as the rest of the team yell playful taunts at him.

6.05pm

Max is outside, hoping that some fresh air will ease his headache. With the exception of his helmet and visor he's in full riot gear now. From the rooftop stadiums he can hear the echo of the Maxie-Mums' chanting – "Maxie, Maxie, he's the man!" He doesn't quite feel like the man any more. He wonders if he has enough money put aside to retire after this season. He knows Glennys will blow a fuse if he flags up the idea.

Now the games umpire is reading out the first recitation of the Revised Riot Act over the public address systems. Ground level TV news reporters with camera crews in tow will be hurriedly squeezing in their last interview with the gangs of youth assembling in the designated riot zone.

Max inhales the muggy air, cursing the fact that the storm he had hoped for didn't materialise. It's going to be hell out there. Riots have no fixed timeframe. This one could easily last to well past midnight. The umpire finishes her announcement and almost immediately Repeet Offenda's "Lootin' on a Saturday Night" comes pounding bass heavy out of the PA. "Here we go looty-loot. Here we go looty-li…"

"You're being set up, Mr Boateng," says a voice from behind a row of rubbish skips.

Max looks up.

"Who's there?"

He knows the man who steps out from behind the skips – Jim Mellish, one of the retired Police Commissioners who sits on Urban Riot's board of directors. Mellish has a polystyrene cup of vending machine coffee in his right hand and a cigarette in his left. He looks at the cigarette. "I should really give these up."

Max walks toward him.

"Stay where you are," he says, taking a step back toward the skips. "I've got something you need to hear. But I'm taking a huge risk. I don't think there's any CCTV back here – but you can never tell."

"What is this?" demands Max. "You come to give me some sort of pep talk?"

"There's something you need to be aware of," says Mellish, dropping the cigarette and crushing it with the sole of his shoe.

Max can hear the crowd joining in with Repeet Offenda's chorus – "Here we go looty-loot. Here we go looty-li."

Mellish blows on his coffee and takes a slow sip.

"Things are not going half as well as they might seem," he continues. "Viewing figures are down. Ticket sales are down. Key sponsors are talking about pulling out next season. My colleagues on the board are getting quite nervous. Some of them have invested considerable sums from their pension pots into the concept of Urban Riot."

"I'm just a cop," says Max. "None of that has anything to do with me. I perform for the crowd. I exceed my arrest targets."

"You're our top cop, Mr Boateng," concedes Mellish. "And that's why you're about to be set up."

Max feels a rush of his blood pounding in his temples. The whistle in his ear is almost painful now. "What are you talking about?" he asks, swaying a little unsteady on his feet.

"Everything has become far too predictable," replies Mellish. "They smash a few windows – we burst a few heads. Then we move the whole circus on to the next fixture - another game, another city. The novelty is wearing off. The excitement is waning. The punters want something to give games the edge they had when they first started. Something big."

"I still don't see what this has to do with me?" says Max.

"What if Britain's top riot cop died during tonight's fixture?" is the unexpected question thrown back at him.

Pride kicks in.

"I've no intention of dying any time soon," he says.

"Who says you have a choice?" asks Mellish. He takes a last mouthful of coffee and tosses the cup into one of the skips. "They've embedded plain clothes operatives into the riot zone. Their job is to entice you away from the main formation. You are to become a martyr, Mr Boateng. They plan to turn the rest of the season into one long grudge match. The National Riot Squad out for revenge for the murder of the nation's hero. They're convinced it will be money spinner."

Max is lost for words. In the thick silence that follows he hears the umpire cut into the Repeet Offenda track and begin her second reading of the Revised Riot Act. He feels his headache intensify. "Why are you telling me this?" he asks.

"Because, unlike my compatriots, I still have some tenuous grasp on my moral compass. This is a step too far for me. It is nothing more than premeditated murder."

Max rubs the heel of his hand against his eye as the whistling in his ear steps up another octave. "So what are you suggesting I do?"

"I'm suggesting you thwart their plan. Tell them you're too sick to go on tonight. From the looks of you it won't be too much of a lie. Use your head, Mr Boateng. Save your own life."

Again Max finds himself stunned into silence.

"Those who do not intend to participate in tonight's riot now have five minutes to vacate the area," announces the umpire. "Once the area is sealed I will then commence the final reading of the Revised Riot Act. Anyone remaining will be considered to be there of his or her own free will and therefore fully cognisant of the consequences."

"I know what you're thinking," says the man. "You've wondering if you should discuss this with you agent. I would suggest that you do not. As one of our major external investors she's been fully appraised of what is being planned and has already engaged the services of a writer and a publisher in order to cash in with a hastily released posthumous biography."

If nothing else that Mellish has told him rings true, this does. The words that Glennys spoke to him when they were on the way back from Lunch with Loretta come back to him now – "You know how much people have got riding on you."

Bitch, he thinks,

When he looks up Mellish is gone.

6:50pm

Max sits at a table in a sports bar a few blocks away from the riot zone. He feels incredibly liberated and light-headed. His headache has eased and his ear is no longer ringing. Even his shoulder seems less stiff. As he'd slipped away from the Bull Ring he'd heard Glennys calling out for him somewhere in the corridors.

"Max? Where the fucking hell are you? What's this bullshit about you not being able to go on?"

He flagged down a taxi before she managed to corner him and switched off his phone when she started ringing it constantly. He isn't planning on switching it back on till he speaks to his accountant in the morning and starts considering his options. He suspects he is going to have to leave the country. It won't be just Glennys who is pissed off at him now and he is certain that Mellish isn't going to risk offering any more assistance.

He takes a sip from his glass of whiskey and pushes his sunglasses back along the bridge of his nose. The bar is packed and he isn't taking any chances on someone recognising him. Not that anyone is paying him any attention. All eyes are on the wall-mounted flat screen TV that is tuned into the live coverage of the riot.

The fixture is in full swing – volleys of petrol bombs – baton charges – close arm to arm combat – shield versus baseball bat. Some cops sustaining minor injuries but mostly the kids in jeans and hoodies coming off worse. A large group or rioters has been kettled into a small area of side streets. Armoured police vehicles are circling in, ready to take delivery when the arrest started being made. The crowds on the rooftop stands are chanting rowdily – "Here we go looty-loot!"

Now the camera pans away from the main action to where a lone rioter is doggedly trying to kick in a shop window. A single riot cop breaks away from the main ranks and runs to intercept him. "This is more like it," yells someone at the bar. "One on one. Go on my son." It isn't clear whether he's rooting for the cop or the rioter.

The camera zooms in on the identification number on the back of the cop's helmet. "47530," says the commentator. "That's PC Shona McLean. Now that Max Boateng is out of the picture she'll be looking to up her arrest rate."

Take your chances while you can, Shona, thinks Max and toasts his glass to the screen. The camera zooms back out. PC McLean raises her baton. The rioter turns and produces something from the belt around his jeans. A handgun. Max remembers the kid who was interviewed on TV that morning and how he boasted that Max was going down.

Shit, he thinks, that was part of the plan and they're still going through with it.

He lets out a yell and jumps to his feet.

"Shut up," someone at the back of the crowd gathered before the screen yells back at him.

Max is frozen to the spot as the dreadful, premeditated execution plays out before him. It's clear to Max now that the supposed rioter is a professional. He knows exactly where to aim. The vulnerable spot around the neck, just above the body armour. Shona McLean's head jerks violently backwards as the bullet penetrates.

"That's fucking out of order!" someone complains loudly.

"Hope they string the bastard up," adds someone else.

Out of the nearby doorways another half a dozen figures appear. Armed with an assortment of weapons they descend upon the body of the woman who will soon be the nation's heroine. The screen cuts to footage of stunned looks on the faces of spectators on the rooftop stands.

Max slumps back into his chair.

"There's going to be hell to pay after this," says the commentator.

COMPETITION

By Diotima Sophia

Competition – it's all about the competition.

It's about the game, the playing.

I'm an addict, and there's no cure.

I have to play. I have to be – playing.

I'm not addicted to gambling, I never bet. I don't play the lottery, I don't go on bingo sites, I've never been in a betting shop. That sort of second-hand playing just doesn't do it for me. I don't care how Tottenham Hotspur do in some tournament or which horse runs faster over a series of fences – because that's not me playing, d'you see? It's got to be me playing, it's got to be my game.

And you'd be surprised just how many times I get to play everyday.

You do, too – I bet you even play some of the same games, you just don't think about it. Simple things – how often do you look across at another driver and think "I can get away before you do, matey!" and expend precious fossil fuels to prove something to yourself?

The thing is – you can't answer that. You don't remember, because you don't care. I do. I've had 25 stop light duels in the last month – and I've won 12 of them. 2 of them I was never going to win – there's no point in trying to outrun boy racers in their souped up cars. Oddly enough, expensive cars like Ferraris never even try – I guess you don't sink that amount of money into a car to pull stunts like that.

Did the other people in the duels notice? I don't care – because the game's not about them, d'you see, it's about me. It's about me, playing and winning. Playing's important but winning is, as well. I know, I know – they all say it's the taking part. But be honest – have you ever known anyone who really believes that, when it's their team, their turn? Nah – they're just like everyone else. It's the playing AND the winning.

Now, you'd think someone like me would have a high falutin' job in the stock market, or play with other people's money in banking or something, right? But like I said – that doesn't work. That's not my money, it's not my game.

No, I have an ordinary, simple job. I work in an office, like almost everyone else I know. I get there in the morning, I do my job, I have lunch, I do more of my job, I leave. But...

Getting there in the morning has its own games. I said above about the stop lights. Then there's the whole parking lot game – can I get closer to the building than I did yesterday? That one has a built in failure rate, because of course the closer I get today, the less chance I have tomorrow of getting even closer. But that's the fun of it – it's a game, d'you see?

Course I try to get in before certain people. Getting in before Jane – she's the big boss – that just doesn't happen. I'm not even sure she goes home. Never beaten her here. But the rest – I've beat 'em all at least once or twice.

And I have rules. I'm honest with my games, I am. No cheating – it's one reason I only play games against myself, cause I'm the only person I know I can trust not to cheat. Well, up till now I've only played against myself, but now... well, I'll get on to that.

So when I talk about getting in before someone else, it only counts if I'm all the way into the main office before they come in the front door – none of this "my foot entered the building first" stuff for me. A good, clear win, that's what I'm after.

And I like to vary it a bit, as well. Sometimes, I try to do something first, like get in in the morning – or need new staples (that's a palaver – all stationery goes through the receptionist now, after someone was caught with a bootful of supplies and an eBay shop – so you have to go to Roxanne and explain what you've done with all the old staples before she'll give you a new box. But she's alright, Roxanne is – you just got to keep on the good side of her).

Sometimes, it's about being the last – that's why this note is written on the back of something that's already been printed. I'm trying to be the last one to need a new box of paper. And I'm probably the only one in the office who knows who's had new paper in the last four months – Roxanne sure doesn't, cause she doesn't care.

It's not a game to her, y'see, like it is to me. And I know, I know that if I can hold out another two, maybe three weeks, old Robinson over there, who never prints anything (because he's usually asleep for half the day) will need more paper and I'll win.

Sure, I could take some of the paper from his stack, but that'd be cheating, see? And I DON'T CHEAT.

Ever.

Not even now.

They said I have a fifty-fifty chance with this disease. I'll get better –
or I won't. It's a game. I won't cheat – all that stuff they're offering me, all
those pills – they've more or less admitted they're not sure they'll work,
or how they work.

So, no – it's just me and this disease. We'll see who wins.

Come back in six months – if I'm here, I'll have won.

And I'll have had to get new paper, by then.

SIMULTOWN

by JP Alders

There was never more a depressing sight than when you walked around Dregerton in the rain.

If you were lucky on some days it was foggy and then you never saw anything. Not that you'd want to spend too much time in this place. The streets weren't awash with people any more. If they wanted to leave the house they went elsewhere to do their shopping. The only real time they went to the centre was at the weekend when the streets were full with people boozing. That's all this once proud city was left with. A couple of hundred years ago the mills kept the city going and to some extent the world, but not any more.

It was certainly a while since Dregerton had a new look. Everybody knew it needed one.

How many pound shops could one city centre hold? In this case there could never be too many. For every pound shop that opened there was always a 99p shop that needed to open as well. If you were to look out of the town hall the view was very grim. To the left hand side there was a pile of rubble where the intended new shopping centre was meant to be. After years of preparation they found the ideal group to fund the idea. It seemed too good to be true; it was. They had the money to knock it all down but they never built anything there.

MONDAY: ABOUT 9am

Mark looked out of the window.

"Ever get the feeling you've been cheated?" he said to the man stood next to him.

"I don't, what you mean by that?" Geoff answered.

"You know it's what Johnny Rotten said to the crowd before the Sex Pistols split up in America," Mark answered.

"No, didn't know that, what do you mean?" Geoff said back to next to him.

"You know we stand here and looks like we've taken part in some war. But we haven't. We just haven't got any money to build anything. Look at Leeds, they just seem to throw money there. What have they ever given us? Apart from Harry Ramsden." Mark asked.

"That's more than we've ever had. What about Marks and Spencer's, weren't they from Leeds?" Geoff asked.

"Yeah that was a long time ago though, probably about the same time when this place was happening," He said before laughing. "Let's go visit the room where all the magic is happening," he said to the man. They entered the room where people were operating several computers. All of them looked to have the city centre on their screens.

"Are these the new plans for the centre? There's no room to put that big wheel you know," he said to them.

"I believe they're playing the latest new game." Geoff said to him.

"Shouldn't they be working on something we can accomplish?" Mark asked.

"I think it may be giving them some ideas to what actually do," Geoff said to him. "What exactly is the game called?"

The people sat in front of the computers didn't turn around. They continued to be engaged with the computer screen.

"I believe it's called Simultown," Geoff answered.

"Hello, young man having fun with the game, is it likely we'll have some work done today. We are under pressure to obtain the best we can with limited resources." Mark asked. the tension visible in his voice. "Yeah it's great I've already knocked down the centre of Stoke to build a new Velodrome." The young man answered.

"Can we make sure that we're actually doing some real designing now, please?" Mark said this at the top of his voice so they could hear his voice all over the room.

The Dog and Gun was one of the few pubs you could drink in the city centre without seeing a fight. They'd capitalised on the real ale trade and dealt with posh food in order to scare the ten pints then home crowd. It was a regular haunt of Mark, where he would go to right the world. He always drank coffee though. Geoff was usually with him. He usually drank a pint instead and joked with Mark about it. "Not having a pint today, not even tempted?" He would say while floating the pint in his face. He would then sip it. "It tastes nice today," he would say to Mark before sipping it up.

"Ah yes, the only boom industry left here, the drinking industry," he said.

He looked over to see a couple of young men engrossed on their phones. They were tapping very fast on them until slamming them down in frustration. "Mustn't be the text they wanted," Mark said to the man behind the bar. "No it's not that. They're playing that new building game." he said. "What new building game? Not that one where they redesign cities?" Mark asked, intrigued. "Yes ,the very one," the man said.

"They do it for phones as well!" Mark answered.

"You can come up with some really good designs. You should try it," the man behind the bar said.

"No, I'm okay thanks. Reminds me too much of work," Mark said back to the man behind the bar.

"You know where I am if you need anybody new for planning," he shouted towards Mark. He picked up that day's new newspaper before sitting down. "What's the world coming to? Next they'll be designing games based on how to arrange the councils accounts and what the money goes towards."

He spotted the newspaper and read the headline. For the first time in months the headline wasn't related to a murder. "Council office leaks plans for new buildings opposite the town hall." Mark stared at the front page before saying, "No murders again, I keep reading to see if it's anyone I know," he said. He looked onto the next page and saw the plans. "It looks quite good, doesn't it?" Mark said, looking towards Geoff. The trainee showed him the image on the computer of the new design. "Here it is," he said. Mark squinted at the screen. "Oh hang on that's an image off the game, I'll just put the proper image up," the trainee said. Mark squinted at the new image. "That looks identical to the last image you showed me," Mark said. "Really, you think so?" the trainee said back to him.

"Yes it looks identical to the last image you showed me, are you sure it's okay?" Mark said. The trainee flicked back to the previous image again. "I'm getting confused with the game; I'll take you through my description." He said. "This big snake shaped thing here, opposite the town hall will be considered the artistic highlight of the north," the trainee said. "What is it going to be called?" Mark asked intrigued. "It will be named the Snake of the North and people will travel for miles just to see it." The trainee proclaimed. "What will it be made of?" Mark asked intrigued. "I'm thinking concrete," the trainee answered. "Concrete! When are you planning to build this? The 1970s. Whats that in front of it?" Mark asked even more intrigued. "That's a water feature. Every centre has got to have a water feature these days. Maximum points on the game it is," the trainee said. "Where do you expect to get the money for the water feature to come from?" asked Mark his head frowning more than normal. "You know the council flats at the edge of town?" the trainee said. "What Everfields, one of the largest council estates in Europe?" Mark said. "Yeah, we knock them down and get someone with independent money to buy the site for a supermarket and that's where we get the money from," the trainee said to him. "Where will the people live that were living in the flats go to live?" said Mark, the anger audible in his voice. "Oh sorry, getting the game mixed up with reality again… but still could we do it?" the trainee asked. "Of course we can't, where would those people live. Could they come and stay around yours?" Mark asked in an angrier tone.

"No of course not, I haven't got any room in my flat and besides I live in Leeds," the trainee answered. "Can we think of proper ideas that we haven't created on a computer now. Take time out of it, it might do you some good," Mark said. "Well there must be an element of truth to it, it's based on real plans for cities," the trainee said.

"Who told you this fact?"

Mark asked, even more intrigued. "It says so at the start of the game. You get maximum points if you send people in council flats to another town. When I play I send them down to London. It's crowded down there, nobody will notice," The trainee said before smiling. "We can't really do that sort of thing in real life I'm afraid. Might lose us some votes," Mark said back to him. "Here's another plan," the trainee said. "I like it, I like this a lot. All these wonderful things within working distance opposite the town hall and there the things people would like. I'll go with it," Mark said. "How do you get hold of this game then?" Mark asked.

"It's quite easy you just type up the name on the internet and the game appears," the trainee answered. His face lit up. It was as if whenever you mentioned the game he woke back up.

"Internet, when was the last time you tried operating a computer?" Geoff said. "I'm just beginning to wonder if it would be worth me looking at what other ideas we could have. This lad is obviously very enthusiastic about it and I want to know why." Mark answered.

"You've not got long left, we'll be finishing in twenty minutes," Geoff said. "It's okay, I'll do it when I get home," he answered.

MONDAY: RUSH HOUR

He drove the long drive home. He passed a few closed-off crime scenes before he arrived back home. His house was situated in the middle of nowhere. Incredibly large for one person to live and quite possibly it had no distractions because of this. Although he had a computer he rarely used it. Before he even switched it on he had to wipe the layer of dust off it.

Mark couldn't remember the last time he had been tempted to play a computer game. Actually he couldn't remember if he'd ever played a computer game. When he looked online he found it quite easy to track down. He also couldn't believe that it was free. Where was the profit in it, he wondered? He looked over it and began to see more people went online and that's where they made their money. He did wonder if his contemporaries in other towns and cities were looking at the game and getting ideas from it. The most distracting thing he could see was the tagline at the top. "Your City Your Vision". Offices all over the land would pay someone an awful lot of money to come up with a phrase like that for where they lived. Before you got to the main game there was a list of top ten places to be rebuilt and comments people had made.

The top five looked awful to him. In the eyes of a modern architect they'd probably look wonderful. "I thought Halifax was just a bank but apparently it's a town. Who would have thought it?" The town centre had money on the trees and everyone was dressed like bankers.

It looked like a weirder version of London except they'd placed a big flag of Yorkshire on the ground. Some of the ideas were weird. One design of London had somewhere in the centre where people could be hanged or shot. They'd looked at the way the acoustics were designed at the O2 Arena and made it that way so no-one could miss a bit.

Some people had decided to completely destroy areas and make the centre completely different. Some city centres were unrecognisable. He used his own name on there and began to rearrange what he thought the centre would look like. He began to learn he was quite a perfection-ist when it came to this sort of thing. He found out early if you built new housing in the fields and surrounding areas you got extra points but he was going to become too consumed by what he could do with the game. He'd always wanted a comedy club. He wouldn't have to drive out of town. Build a wall around all the dodgier parts of town be able to keep the less nice individuals stuck in one place. Be able to cut down on policing then.

Save money there and one of them can stand on the door to protect the town hall and then people won't be able to attack them for their decisions. There's no mention of how much bullet proof windows cost, they could do with some of them as well. Building a special tunnel to the wonderful things opposite. That way they could get in and out of there quicker.

Up to date CCTV to get footage of who it is trying to attack the building. Unemployment wouldn't matter as they would be in prison. All this would lead to maximum points.

Nationally it would look like unemployment had gone down in the city and there would be new places for unemployment for the people who lived there. As he looked out of the window, daylight had begun to appear. He set the alarm and slept in the chair with his clothes still on.

TUESDAY: MORNING

When he arrived at work the television was on. He couldn't believe they were mentioning the very computer game he had been playing. The news channel were showing the new design for the port of Southampton. The voice on the television was waffling on about how realistic it looked. They didn't mention the men on the top of the wall with the guns were a step too far. "We could do with one of those here on a Saturday night, or the police with rubber bullets." A chorus of voices echoed throughout the room. As the interview continued the person being interviewed kept barraging the interviewee with various comments about how many points something is. "Those southerners don't know what they're doing as per usual, it would never happen up here," he said. As he looked around the room the staff were on the computers looking at designs of the game. If you were to look at the room it was filled with computers which just featured computer generated images of various cities. The game was clearly getting onto all the machines. Mark sat down and began to look at the computer.

"What are you doing?" Geoff said. "You know I'm just looking for more ideas." Mark looked at the screen and began to get frustrated by the game when he saw other cities were getting ahead of him. "I'm doing everything right, how can I not be in the top ten list of people?" He said out aloud. As he mentioned this an advert appeared in the corner for a guide for the game. It kept flashing up saying buy the guide it was reasonably priced. If you want to build the city of the future. New York, London, and then a question mark for wherever the player was going to build. He picked up the phone and dialled up Geoff even though he was stood behind him. The phone rang and Geoff picked it up. "Hello," Geoff said to the phone. "Yeah I'm going go out for a bit, got to a buy a book, Geoff, can you look after the office for me?"

He asked down the phone. "What do you mean I could have told you that, I'm busy on the computer can't you see?" Geoff put down the phone and wandered over to where Mark was sat. "Are you to going to buy the book then?" Geoff asked as Mark just stared at the screen.

"Yeah I'm just going to leave now, don't touch the computer!" he yelled towards Mark before storming off outside. As he wandered down the street he tried to find the game on the phone but it just wasn't advanced enough to do anything. You could ring people up on it.

This didn't stop people eye him up down the street. His phone wasn't that good or even that up to date but if the people of Dregerton could get something for free they would.

As he wandered into the shop he didn't have time to read the badly-spelt graffiti or even notice the boarded-up window such was the excitement of getting the book. The assistant working there wandered over in what appeared to be a stabproof vest. They clearly had no idea who Geoff was. "Have you a guide for Simultown?" Mark asked. The assistant looked at him before getting a copy of it. "Think it's what our council need." the assistant said. "I can remember when this was the place to be, but not anymore," the assistant said before their eyes glazed over. He saw the price of the book was a reasonably priced 60 pound.

He knew it was clearly worth every penny. He didn't even acknowledge the person who had served him before rushing out of the shop. He got the book out of the bag and started reading the back of it. Not only did it give top tips for your city it also gave you examples of places that had benefitted from the game. Pudsey was just a market town until town planners got hold of this game and now look at it. It's a market town of the future. Who remembers Pudsey before we build the ski slope in the centre? Nobody. That's what Simultown does to your town. There were even quotes from MPs and members of local councils on there. "We thought we lived in a tired, dead, depressing dreary place where the only exciting thing that happened was when the sun came out until we discovered Simultown and now it's sunny every day." His phone began to ring. He looked at it and it was Geoff. "Where are you, you've been gone forty minutes." Mark had managed to find himself sat on a bench reading the book. "Just been reading a book about town planning," Mark answered. "You can always do that when I get back," Geoff growled down the line. "I'll just be ten minutes," He said before hanging up. He sat down another ten minutes before picking it up and reading it some more.

The bench he was sat on was outside the council house. Within five minutes he wandered back in straight past people in the office and sat in front of the computer. "Are we not going to have a meeting today then?" Geoff asked. Mark just looked at him and then looked at the computer and picked the book up. "I'll best make us a brew then," Geoff said. For the rest of the day Geoff sat behind Mark as he tried various different ideas. Now and again he would inform him that wasn't his job but he didn't listen. Apart from the odd swear word all he kept saying was "If we combine the designs with the trainee we could come up with something good."

"We'll have to build a car park there otherwise how are people going to get here?"

Was the only reply Geoff said. When it actually got to five o'clock Geoff left Mark in the office still on the computer game.

WEDNESDAY: 9:00am

When Geoff arrived at work the following morning he was pleasantly surprised. Mark wasn't sat at the computer and was staring into space. "Do you know what I might do today?" Mark said. "Not play that computer game?" was Geoff's answer. "No, I think we should all take a meeting down the pub." he answered. "So you've finally got everything to do with that computer game out of your system then?" He asked. Mark's face looked thoughtful before saying "While Simultown like that you enjoy playing their game they recommend you take at least eight hours sleep every night as this is what real town planners do and from time to time they recommend you take meetings in the pub." "Is that you saying that or the game?" Geoff asked. Either way they wandered down to the pub where they were to have their meeting. "Bit early for my pint today isn't it?" Geoff said to the people there as if he needed to confirm it out loud. "Bit early Geoff, how do you take your coffee?" Mark said. "Does this mean I won't be able to have a pint later?" Geoff said the expression on his face still clearly showing that he wanted a drink. "We might come back later, how would you like your coffee?" Mark asked again. Geoff smiled back at him. "Can I have a strong one then please, by that I mean a coffee and not an alcoholic beverage," He answered with his voice getting higher at the end. "That's more like it," Mark said grinning. They'd also brought along the new trainee who was consistently playing with his phone. "Can you pay attention please?"

Mark said to the trainee who looked at him a bit blank and then continued to play with his phone. "Hey you're not playing that game on your phone are you?" Mark asked with a glint in his eye. "I was playing it last night, did quite well," Mark said. "You played the game. How well did you do?" the trainee asked intrigued. "That's why I'm taking this meeting now," Mark answered. "No really how well did you do?" the trainee asked. "Actually I did pretty well, I found a new idea for opposite the town hall. "Have you ever tried building an escape route for when people try to come and burn the town hall down?" Mark answered him. "Oh yes, do you realise you get extra points for that as well. The tunnels can be used for tourist purposes in the future." the trainee answered. "I knew that but I didn't realise it was a multipurpose idea," Mark nodded, looking very interested. Geoff looked at them both blankly.

"I don't understand the obsession you have with this computer game, Mark. You always used to say to me people who played computer games were more braindead than zombies," Geoff said. Mark turned his head around and gave Geoff a look. "This game's different though," he said. "You also said if I ever find you playing such a game I've to thrown a glass of water in your face, shake you and say to you, what are you doing man?" Geoff answered before continuing "Isn't it a bit like doing your work at home though?" He said. "No it's really good for idea generation," Mark answered.

"Seems a waste of time to me." Geoff said. "But it's not, it's really good," the trainee said to them. "Is there anything realistically we can build off it?" Geoff asked. "Of course, it's all based in reality. I've seen casinos that go on for 15 miles in America." the trainee answered.

Geoff pulled a face. "That might work well in America but we haven't got that sort of room here, and where would we get the money from?" Geoff was pulling a face. "Aren't you going to say anything about this Mark? You're usually the one questioning this kind of thing?"

"Like the man said, these things are possible."

"Two words for you: independent funding," the trainee said. "You get extra points for that", the trainee said. "You also get extra points for training someone new on the game as well Geoff, so guess what you'll be doing next."

Geoff's face dropped before replying, "No, it's never too early for a pint."

Geoff had been sat in front of the computer for a couple of hours now. "How do you do this again?" He asked to the room who were now absorbed in what was happening on their monitors. "Just a minute Geoff, we're trying to read what the number for the independent funding is on one of these buildings." "It's not real Mark," Geoff answered to Mark.

"Everything included in the game is real, it tells you that at the beginning. As well as no town planners were hurt in the construction of the game," he added. "Don't you think you're taking this game a bit too seriously," Geoff replied. "At this moment in time we need all the help we can to regenerate the area." Mark said. "Come over here and look what we've done to the city," Mark said. Geoff and the rest of the room wandered over and looked at the city.

The trainee simply proclaimed "That's 20 squillion points, you'll be top of the scoring league with that." "That's it then. First we'll ring up the number and then we'll do a press conference then," Mark said. "Sounds great," the trainee said. "Hang on, I've missed what's going on here," Geoff said. "It's quite simple really, there's a number that exists on the game and like everything on it, it's real so we've rung it up and they're funding it," the trainee said.

"Hang on, when am I going to be consulted about this?" Geoff said. "It all got done while you were working out how to play the game," Mark answered. "How?" Geoff said. "I was talking on the phone while playing." he said before continuing. "Going to get a press conference organised this afternoon and I'll be able to show people the plans then." he said. The room went silent before the trainee said, "I bet you get a few thousand points for that".

WEDNESDAY: ABOUT 2:00 IN THE AFTERNOON

For a press conference it was very well attended. Mark was sat with his computer in front of him just in case he missed anything on the game. "If you were to say to me twelve months ago people actually wanted to develop things here. That I'd be playing a computer game for ideas I'd say you were mad. But here it is the plan and as you can see anything's possible," Mark said.

"Where are you getting the money from?" one voice in the room said. "No need to worry, all the money is coming from independent sources. We won't be raising the tax in any way shape or form." "Can we quote you on that," another voice in the room said. "Oh yes, we've looked into independents funds." Mark answered. "Yes we're using a company we've seen on the game, they exist and they are very good. They're called Scarpaite Building," Mark said.

The room was full of grumbles. "Do you realise how ridiculous that sounds," one of the journalists said. "Now you may think it's a ridiculous idea but we all know it will work in the council office. You have my word on this. Dregerton will enter a new term of prosperity."

With that he showed the plan to the room. It was greeted with the sound of booing. "What about Loughborough?" another of the journalists asked. "What about it?" He answered.

"They followed the same game and turned the area into one large rubbish tip. There was a glitch in the system and planners thought they could get maximum points. Nothing going on there. Who'd want to visit the biggest rubbish tip in Europe?" the journalist finished. There was a small silence before the reply. "They do things different in the south." Mark knew sometimes you just had to ignore public opinion. Besides he needed to get back to his game.

He was sure he could beat his new score.

Months passed and seasons changed yet the fog and general mugginess remained even in the height the summer when it had been the hottest day on record. It was around then that the building opposite finished and the people weren't very happy about it. They hadn't decided on independent funding in the end, they just increased the council tax a lot. Mark looked out of the window while people threw objects at the building. The newly constructed concrete snake now had graffiti all over it. The massive crack in the main window distorted the image from outside but added character Mark thought. "What are we going to do?" Geoff answered.

"Looks like we'll have to wait until it finishes," Mark said. "Guess so, it's not our fault the people building the escape route went bankrupt before they finished." "What are going to do?" Geoff asked. Mark said down and put the computer on. "I'm going to see how I can correct the road system in Birmingham," he said. Geoff looked out of the window. The fantastic row of shops opposite the building remained empty while the coming soon retail units now had rude drawings painted on it. Half of the water feature wasn't working. "Don't think these were the ideal ideas we wanted," Geoff said looking out of the window. "Think the skyscraper with the airport was a bit too much and as for the swimming pool on top who's going want to go up there in rainy Dregerton?" The flames came from under the ground directly outside the building setting the incoming invaders on fire. "Think the fire feature outside the building works just fine," he shouted to Mark in the other room.

TOAD BASEBALL

By Beau Johnson

I was eleven when I accidentally killed my younger brother.

This is not the type of thing one hopes for while growing up, but there it is all the same, the power of it draining, drawn from me like a knife that eats at memory, the boy who was my twin.

I would say it defined me as well. How could it not?

Born John and Jason, we came into the world six minutes apart on the working side of West Virginia – two brothers, the McBlains, wailing at the world from the onset; two brothers awake and there to stay. This is what I tell myself whenever I think of the time we had together, there before it began – before I realized just how small we really, truly are.

Both of our parents were hard-working and both of them held jobs. Mom ironed all day for the upper class, the dividing line of our town being Brock, which ran all the way down to Carrington. Dad was factory, pressing pipe until the fumes ate what lungs the place had left him to live his days with. We never wanted is what I'm saying. That is not to say that we were rich, not in the monetary way. They loved us is all, and both of us loved them – until what happened happened, of course.

It wasn't like I could blame them either. Emotionally I was old enough to understand where they were coming from. Hell, I hated me! Wanted nothing more than the power to wring my own neck as punishment for what I'd done. It didn't happen, of course, but boy had I wanted it. Years later, I continued to want it, but not as much as that first year; in time learning how to contain the self-hatred that seethed within me, allowing it to simmer and no more than that for the waking hours of my day.

Night was a different beast altogether, chock full of all the ingredients every nightmare needs. They lessened as the years wore on, but they never went away, not fully. Sometimes I am in these dreams and sometimes I am on the outside looking in, as if in the third person. Jason is always there, every time, and so is the blood I took from him. He never speaks to me, not with his mouth. He usually just stands there on the patio and stares as the blood from the wound (a wound which, in the dream, has always been more exaggerated than it was in real life) at the side of his head slowly slides towards the ground where it will clump and collect like red cottage cheese. His eyes are empty in this dream, big white O's that look right through me. Occasionally he will lift his arm and point towards something I never see. They are odd, these dreams, and I would be a liar if I said they no longer affect me.

So yes, I would say ending my brother's life holds a part in defining me. Hell, you could even argue it created someone altogether new. And for the record, I did not mean to, not ever, but it still does not change the fact that my hands were the ones swinging the bat that day.

Our backyard was small. Tiny, really, and almost identical to every other in the row of townhouses in which we lived. On either side of the sliding patio doors were window wells, each about three feet deep. They held stones, gravel and the like at the bottom, forming a kind of bed. These window wells would sometimes hold toads as well, the creatures getting in there and nestling for warmth between what rocks they could negotiate. It is because of these toads that Jason and I were outside of our backyard that day – a place we both knew we should never go, not without some sort of protection. Be it father, mother, or tactical nuke.

His name was Rodney Bowers. He was the block bully, and man did he live up to his name. A terror, really, and large for his age, which seems to be the way it goes, no? With bullies, I mean, that they always seem big for their age; perhaps that's why they become bullies in the first place – too much mass and not enough brains to fill in the requisite space. To go with his size Rodney had a shovel for a face, wide, with his chin ending in somewhat of a point. Small beady eyes overlooked a flat nose covered in freckles. He wore overalls too, if that helps set the scene.

And we knew to steer clear, all of us; knew that Rodney and his band of terrors ruled the roost and woe betide the child crossing him and his boys coming to or from school, or just around the block. His cohorts were smaller than him, but no less mean – sometimes meaner if given the chance. They were the Brady boys, Randy and Jeff, each brother not much more than a puddle in t-shirts and jeans. A year apart, they shared the same sense of god-awful humour – the type which seemed to laugh at a joke far too hard for far too long. They were nowhere near as funny as they thought they were either. But underneath that laughter laid mean-ness, as I have already mentioned. It was bone deep in those two, double sharp and quick to cut. I have often believed that as Rodney became entwined with these two… that he was nothing more than accelerant to an already burning flame. Time would tell, and did. But that was after, near the end of their lives.

It is before I would like to discuss; that Rodney, Randy and Jeff were such tyrants that lunch money would be given over without even being asked for; that kids would push over one another to get out the door once the bell rang just to sprint their entire way home. They wanted no piece of what Rodney brought, no taste of what his Kingship decreed. And who could blame them? We were smaller, weaker, each of us struggling to survive not only the current day at hand but what we knew to be coming: high school. Where bullies like Rodney became a dime a dozen, each a leader to the pack they chose. It would only get worse for kids like Jason and me. The way the world worked and had worked since time out of mind. Welcome to wonderland, people! Hang on to your hats and leave your money at the door!

He'd made a kid eat his own feces once – this being the story that stuck; the one which made the legend. After this the block became Rodney's, and more or less the school. Adam Clarke, who became Shitbreath after the fact, had been the unfortunate soul in the washroom that day. In the first floor lavatory this was, between the fourth graders and the fifth. You would think something like this couldn't happen, not in elementary school, a civilized place of four hundred kids. Not too big a number, nor too small. You would think a boy who had to move his bowels would be able to do so without fear of having to chew it up and re-swallow it down in front of a captive, laughing, guffawing audience of three. You would, wouldn't you? Not where Jason and I grew up. Not even close.

Poor kid had braces, too – the large kind, solar system and all.

Which more or less brings me back to the toads and the day we found them; back to the day when my brother's heart came shining through.

He always liked animals, always, ever since we were small. Dogs, cats, birds, what have you. It didn't matter. Be it insects or fish, spiders or frogs. He loved them all, always giving whatever creature catching his attention the best of what he was.

"How do you think they got in there?" This is what Jason asked me once we discovered the toads in the window well that day. I had no concrete answer for him – the well appearing much too high for a toad to climb. I suggested they burrowed their way in from somewhere we couldn't see. This seemed to appease him. It did not deter him from freeing them, however, which had become the goal the moment he noticed them.

"What if they starve," was his argument. I could not disagree with him. Nine toads later, all of them secured in mother's Tupperware, our quest began.

I must stop here, and only for a moment. I wish to stress how much my brother loved animals. I know I have already mentioned this, but I don't know if I have explained it as fully as I could have. We had a dog once, a puppy. It developed cancer. Jason slept with that dog for three months straight while it succumbed. My parents finally had to take it away from him as the disease brought the dog close to the end. Jason would have none of it. He kicked and screamed, he cried and raged. It was his dog, his, and he was the one meant to help it home. I didn't understand what he was saying at the time, not then. But I came to, years later, realizing just how mature my brother had been for his age. I think he thought he could heal, or that he was meant to be a protector of some kind. I'll never know, not for sure, but it's what I try to tell myself whenever the blackouts return.

Toads in Tupperware, we ventured out from the backyard, towards Rodney and his pals, though we didn't yet know it. We should have though, seeing as we had been living in fear of them for the better part of three years.

"Well whadda-ya-know! It's the freakin' Bobsi twins!" Rodney exclaimed, his bushy brows gathering into the usual position. The one that says it is time to play, fuck you or otherwise. Immediate laughter followed this – the braying kind, from both Randy and Jeff. What came next was Rodney noticing what Jason held within his hands.

"What-choo got there, retard?" Rodney Bowers, ladies and gentlemen – the apex of our race.

"Toads." Jason said, no more. And to tell you the truth, I was surprised he had said anything at all. If there was one difference between my brother and me, it was this: I was the braver one. I do not say this to gloat. I say it simply as fact. I also do not say this to suggest I wasn't scared of Rodney – quite the opposite, as a matter of fact. It's that I have a line, and afraid or not, pushed hard enough, I will push on back. Fight or flight I believe it's called. Still, I should have realized.

"I can see that, numb-nuts. What? You don't think I can see!?" And there it was – what all bullies live and breathe on. They make it about themselves, projecting whatever junk they have on the inside onto whatever is readily available. They are self-loathers, each and every one.

"No; that's not what I said." Besides what his words represented, I think it was a combination of them and what Rodney's eyes did – how they widened in disbelief – that caused my jaw to hit the ground. To be honest, it was amazing. My brother never showing me what he showed me that Saturday afternoon, never once in his too short life. Randy and Jeff stood exactly the same, their mouths replicas of mine, and perhaps time stood still there for a second or two, or perhaps it did not. Either way, the moment broke, replaced by an anger we knew all too well.

"Alright, fuck-o – you want to play, we can play!" Randy and Jeff came forward at that, as if soldiers at attention, but soldiers with greasy hair and unbrushed teeth. They had ball gloves as well, hanging from their hips, and in Randy's hand was the bag which contained their bats and balls. I then realized how we'd run into them; that the ball diamond was on the other side of the road past the end of our parking lot. They had been on their way to play a game, the two of us landing right in their way. As ever, I was a second too slow in registering what Rodney was about to do, but I saw it all in slow-motion once it began; saw him ask Randy for a bat; saw Randy give him one as Jeff snatched the Tupperware container from out of Jason's hands; watched Rodney state that it was time for he and his friends to play a little of what he liked to call toad-baseball; saw him take up a toad, a larger one, watched him loft it into the air; listened to him shout "Batters up!" as he began to swing, his body all torque, his body coming round. Connecting, time turned normal, or seemed to, and the guts of the toad struck my face, entered my mouth. I was dumbfounded, shocked, but it was nothing compared to seeing my brother go at Rodney the way that he did.

It was a sight to behold. And I mean that, truly. Primal will be the word I use, because that's what I feel I saw.

He went to town on Rodney, first hitting him in the nuts and then right to his face as the bigger boy went down. The reason it worked was because it was the last thing Rodney expected. We were shorter than he remember, by a foot, each of us fifty pounds lighter. Not to mention the fact that he'd had the neighbourhood by the balls for the better part of

three years. I imagine it was new to him. What he was feeling, I mean –
because that's what I saw in the widening of his eyes: fear; big and round,
dilated and yellow.

If only Randy and Jeff hadn't been there that day, then everything
would have turned out differently. They were there however; each of
them equal in becoming Rodney's saving grace.

They pulled Jason off their leader, scratching and clawing like girls.
They grabbed and hit, they kicked and spat. Not until Rodney himself
stood back up did it all turn to shit. Up, he went at my brother, sneering,
hitting him hard in the gut not once, but twice. It was as he punched
Jason in the face that I exploded; when I unleashed an amount of anger
I have yet to feel again.

We were not angry children, neither of us. I want you to know this.
It was the situation is all, and more than likely the entire three years
prior; the whole time we had been subjected to the evil that was Rodney
Bowers coming to a head right there on the dried out grass not thirty feet
from the backyard we never should have left.

Bending down, I picked up the bat.

Going forward, I increased my pace.

Screaming, I swung.

Whenever I look back on that moment many things go through my
mind. Not only what happened, but how I see it happen; how it seems
I now see it as I sometimes see myself in dreams, from that third person
point of view. Years are the answer for this, I suppose; how time can be
known to wear down a memory if it so chooses, fading it into a former
version of itself. True or not, it is as clear as my picture comes when
I think of that day.

I am swinging full bore. Not for Rodney's head, but for his shoulder.
He is hurting my brother. I only want him to stop. I swing and I swing
and again it all seems to slow down on me; the swing I have begun is the
only one I ever take. I continue to swing, to swing that same swing, and
then slowly I begin to see Rodney move, to pull back and evade. Doing
so, the bat misses him, but continues on the arc I have placed it on.
I continue to swing, momentum imprisoning me. Too late, I realize I am
powerless to stop what is about to occur.

The doctors tell us it was a perfect strike, or as close to a combination
of a perfect strike as one could come; that the way Jason had been bent

down, his head just past Rodney's hip – that the arc of the bat and the angle of his head…

Flush, the bat splits him open at the right temple. Brick-like, he crumbles to the ground like a building coming down.

I don't remember much after that. Not where Randy and Jeff and Rodney ran off to. Not how much time elapsed before our parents found us in the grass, one of their sons cradling the other in such a way as to make their mother scream until her voice runs dry. I don't remember any of those things, not one. What I do recall is feeling Jason die. Down the middle of my head, as the bat collided, I remember a snap, a crack – a split inside my mind. I don't have the words to fully describe what this was. It was there though, like a line of white pain running from the back of my head to the front. First time I felt anything like that, ever. With some twins it is said they can read each other's thoughts, know what the other is thinking – that they are that entwined. Jason and I didn't run like this, not once. What happened when he died was new. This is also what the doctors believed to be the cause of my blackouts.

They don't happen so much anymore, not like they did during that first couple of years after Jason died. One moment I would be watching Little House on the Prairie and the next I would find myself sitting outside the arcade down beside the plaza. People saw me. Even said I spoke with them when my parents really began to dig at why this was happening to me. Both the psychologist and psychiatrist they sent me to eventually told them (in better terms than this) to let it ride; that it was more than possible that this was just my way of dealing with the guilt. Made sense to me; made sense to them. We still moved however, despite the blackouts decreasing in frequency.

Littleton is where we ended up, the big city just north of New Dumfries and the life my parents wished to leave behind. Things improved with time, as things often have a habit of doing. Time heals all wounds, right? This is what they say. I can't say I totally buy into such a thing, but I will say it is something to consider when the bleakness sets in and all seems lost. My blackouts? Regrettably, they remained a part of my life for quite some time, but continued to lessen the older I became. Between episodes, three years was the longest I went without losing time. This was during my sophomore year. Unfortunately, this was also the time the murders began.

Was it me? The unknown person of interest they labeled the Campus Killer? I don't know and can't say with any degree of certainty. What I can let you know is this – it was Rodney Bowers who had caused my (then) latest blackout; that me running into him on campus nine years removed from the day with the toads sparked what I think I have secretly feared since the moment Jason died.

Walking home from chem-lab was when it happened, and he noticed me before I could notice him. He had a beard now, close cut and red. His face was no longer a child's, not puffy nor chunky nor young. Nevertheless, it held the shape I remembered it having. Not as pointy at the chin, but still as overly wide. His eyes remained exactly the same however, small and hateful – a thing I have never forgotten. Eyes like that never change, not once they've matched the heart within.

"Well isn't it one half of the Smothers Brothers! What's up, baby killer? How you been?" It must have been my face, what he registered on it. From the moment he said it, you could see he wished he could retract the words. After that I can tell you nothing. Not for an entire two week period. Oh, I have speculations, don't you worry – as well as assumptions. I can prove nothing, of course, not without admitting to something I am not even sure I have been a part of.

He'd been murdered, you see: Rodney. He and three others, all women, during a span of time I have yet to regain. The position this put me in... I would wish it on no one. Not only because of the history Rodney and I shared, but because of his cause of death: blunt force trauma to the base of the neck. Some type of heavy instrument bashing in the back of his skull.

It had echoes, you see – shades of a bloody, if not symmetrical, past.

I was never questioned, not once, and the killings ended as abruptly as they began – what the papers printed repeatedly as the months wore on. Was it another coincidence? Blind luck that Rodney had chosen to enrol in the very same university as the kid whose brother he helped to inadvertently kill? In another city fifty miles removed from where no one knew of the connection which bound us? Perhaps, but no, I do not believe it. Not so much and not anymore. The reason for this was because of what I found in my basement not a month ago. I share this house with my wife and our twin two-year old girls. New Dumfries is the town we now live in, the same New Dumfries my parents moved me from all those years ago. We have been here four years now, the clinic I opened the reason and choice.

What I found was a collection of ball bats in a bag behind the furnace. They were not new, these bats. They were old, used. They were stained as well, with little chunks of god knows what sticking to the ends.

This was not my bag; one I do not remember purchasing. This means next to nothing of course, as I have lost more time than I care to remember (or not remember, because really, how would I know?) as the days of my life progressed. Not large amounts in the scheme of things, no, but enough if I am to be honest, the incidents growing with some regularity at about the time we moved back here. This is what scares me now, when I look back over my life, especially since Jason's death. I think of that split a lot, that feeling I had the moment he died. It led me places I never thought I would go; the library, for one, and its research rooms, for another. I wanted answers, you see, definitive and concrete. Did I get them? Depends on how you look at it.

Broken down, Twin to Twin Transferral Syndrome is when one twin steals from another without knowing they are doing so. Blood for instance, where one twin, usually the bigger of the two, hoards much of the supply, thereby ensuring his identical brother or sister is born smaller. Intriguing, no? Perhaps when I finish putting it in perspective, then.

I was the bigger twin; what my mother always told us. Keeping in mind TTTS, what if such a thing could continue outside the womb? Insane, right? Of course it is. Does that make it any less plausible?

What if at the moment of Jason's death – what if I did the very same thing I did when we were still inside our mother? And what if instead of absorbing his blood, I took on his soul? It would explain some things. Like how I can miss weeks at a time but everyone I come in contact with during that time admits to noticing nothing out of the ordinary about me. How can that be? Unless someone more than a little like me...someone who might be identical to me in almost every conceivable way...

Also, remember how I told you that Jason liked animals – that he loved them?

I graduated a veterinarian for God's sake! A vet! Does one need any more proof? Okay. Last bit of information and then I will go. And this is the part which has been keeping me up at night; the stuff that turns my stomach so cold I can sometimes taste it at the back of my throat.

The baseball bats, of course – the means by which Jason died. Can you imagine the anger one would have as that happened? The rage it would create the instant before you died? I know I can, being as I was the one who was there. But it's the tapes which are freaking me out! There are two of them now, both of them in the bag of bats and both of then marked WATCH ME. I did not put them there, and only one had been in there when I first found the bag. I know who it is. Deep down, I really do. But do I want to talk to him? That is the question, and the one which begs it all. In the end, who am I really: the shadow of a boy long past gone or, quite simply, my own fractured self?

Does it make sense to you; how my life appears? Would you tell me if it did? Seriously, I am running out of options here. I mean, when I start to think I feel him moving around up there, what's a man to do? Seriously, what does something like this say about a person? What can it?

I love my daughters and my wife. If anything, I will always have that.

DEATH BY SCRABBLE

By Charlie Fish

It's a hot day and I hate my wife.

We're playing Scrabble. That's how bad it is. I'm 42 years old, it's a blistering hot Sunday afternoon, and all I can think of to do with my life is play Scrabble.

I should be out, doing exercise, spending money, meeting people. I don't think I've spoken to anyone except my wife since Thursday morning. On Thursday morning I spoke to the milkman.

My letters are crap.

I play, appropriately, BEGIN. With the N on the little pink star. Twenty-two points.

I watch my wife's smug expression as she rearranges her letters. Clack, clack, clack. I hate her. If she wasn't around, I'd be doing something interesting right now. I'd be climbing Mount Kilimanjaro. I'd be starring in the latest Hollywood blockbuster. I'd be sailing the Vendée Globe on a 60-foot clipper called New Horizons – I don't know, but I'd be doing something.

She plays JINXED, with the J on a double-letter score. 30 points. She's beating me already. Maybe I should kill her.

If only I had a U, then I could play MURDER. That would be a sign. That would be permission.

I start chewing on my H. It's a bad habit, I know. All the letters are frayed. I play WARMER for 22 more points, mainly so I can keep chewing on my H.

As I'm picking new letters from the bag, I find myself thinking – the letters will tell me what to do. If they spell out KILL, or STAB, or her name, or anything, I'll do it right now. I'll finish her off.

My rack spells MIUZPA. Plus the H in my mouth. Damn.

The heat of the sun is pushing at me through the window. I can hear buzzing insects outside. I hope they're not bees. My cousin Harold swallowed a bee when he was nine, his throat swelled up and he died. I hope that, if they are bees, they fly into my wife's throat.

She plays SWEATIER, using all her letters. 24 points plus a 50 point bonus. If it wasn't too hot to move I would strangle her right now.

I am getting sweatier. It needs to rain, to clear the air. As soon as that thought crosses my mind, I find a good word. HUMID on a double-word score, using the D of JINXED. The H makes a little splash of saliva when I put it down. Another 22 points. I hope she has lousy letters.

She tells me she has lousy letters. For some reason, I hate her more.

She plays FAN, with the F on a double-letter, and gets up to fill the kettle and turn on the air conditioning.

It's the hottest day for ten years and my wife is turning on the kettle. This is why I hate my wife. I play ZAPS, with the Z doubled, and she gets a static shock off the air conditioning unit. I find this remarkably satisfying.

She sits back down with a heavy sigh and starts fiddling with her letters again. Clack clack. Clack clack. I feel a terrible rage build up inside me. Some inner poison slowly spreading through my limbs, and when it gets to my fingertips I am going to jump out of my chair, spilling the Scrabble tiles over the floor, and I am going to start hitting her again and again and again.

The rage gets to my fingertips – and passes. My heart is beating. I'm sweating. I think my face actually twitches. Then I sigh, deeply, and sit back into my chair. The kettle starts whistling. As the whistle builds it makes me feel hotter.

She plays READY on a double-word for 18 points, then goes to pour herself a mug of tea. No, I do not want one.

I steal a blank tile from the letter bag when she's not looking, and throw back a V from my rack. She gives me a suspicious look. She sits down with her tea, making a cup-ring on the table, as I play an 8-letter word: CHEATING, using the A of READY. 64 points, including the 50-point bonus, which means I'm beating her now.

She asks me if I cheated.

I really, really hate her.

She plays IGNORE on the triple-word for 21 points. The score is 153 to her, 155 to me.

The steam rising from her cup of tea makes me feel hotter. I try to make murderous words with the letters on my rack. If only there was some way for me to get rid of her.

I spot a chance to use all my letters. EXPLODES, using the X of JINXED. 72 points. That'll show her.

As I put the last letter down, there is a deafening bang and the air conditioning unit fails.

My heart is racing, but not from the shock of the bang. I don't believe it – but it can't be a coincidence. The letters made it happen. I played the word EXPLODES, and it happened – the air conditioning unit exploded. And before, I played the word CHEATING when I cheated. And ZAP when my wife got the electric shock. The words are coming true. The letters are choosing their future. The whole game is – JINXED.

My wife plays SIGN, for 10 points.

I have to test this.

I have to play something and see if it happens. Something unlikely, to prove that the letters are making it happen. My rack is ABQYFWE. That doesn't leave me with a lot of options. I start frantically chewing on the B.

I play FLY, using the L of EXPLODES. I sit back and close my eyes, waiting for the sensation of rising up from my chair. Waiting to fly.

Stupid. I open my eyes, and there's a fly. Buzzing around above the Scrabble board, surfing the thermals from the tepid cup of tea. That proves nothing. The fly could have been there anyway.

I need to play something unambiguous. Something that cannot be misinterpreted. Something absolute and final.

My wife plays CAUTION, using a blank tile for the N. 18 points.

My rack is AQWEUK, plus the B in my mouth. I am awed by the power of the letters, and frustrated that I cannot wield it. Maybe I should cheat again, and pick out the letters I need to spell SLASH or SLAY.

Then it hits me. The perfect word. A powerful, dangerous, terrible word.

I play QUAKE for 19 points.

I wonder if the strength of the quake will be proportionate to how many points it scored. I can feel the trembling energy of potential in my veins. I am commanding fate. I am manipulating destiny.

My wife plays CHOKE for 28 points, just as the room starts to shake.

I gasp with surprise and vindication – and the B that I was chewing on gets lodged in my throat. I try to cough. My face goes red, then blue. My throat swells. I draw blood clawing at my neck. The earthquake builds to a climax.

I fall to the floor. My wife just sits there, watching.

PLAYERS

by Adam Craig

The day Patterson was lost was the day Scott nailed the Virtuex account down dead. Temperley had him stand at the end of the office while the others gathered around.

"A real example of go-get business." Temperley clutched his shoulder with a fatherly hand. "An example to you all."

Scott thought he did a good job with his expression: just the right amount of humility to modulate the pride, and no hint of triumphalism that might blowback unexpectedly. Behind this mask, he studied the faces of his colleagues. Tallying up the signs of envy or jealousy, gauging where each placed him. It looked pretty good. Except one face was missing.

"And," Temperley continued, pumping Scott's hand with manly vigour, "this will earn you a whacking bonus, Scott m'boy."

Temperley said things like that. Somehow he got away with it. But then, he was an experienced player.

Scott promised he wouldn't chuck the lot in one go, then gave a carefully judged bow as everyone dutifully applauded. Again, enough humility to make sure he didn't earn any new enemies, leavened with a pinch of arrogance to get up the nose of his closest competitors. Another look around as he straightened.

No, definitely one face missing.

Scott wasn't going to let it spoil the moment. He took a slow, apparently innocent, wander between the desks and cubicles dotting the open-plan office. Judging and scoring the congratulations he picked up along the way. Eventually, the circuit brought him to the coffee machine at the far end of the room. Masked by a display of potted ferns, he took out his smartphone and began adding up. Stylus tack-ing across the screen, Scott quickly saw he had done even better than he had thought. By his reckoning, he'd manoeuvred himself into a fairly safe position.

"Yes–!"

"Hey, well done."

Scott jumped, guiltily hiding the phone behind his back before seeing it was Snell talking to him.

"Really." Snell held out his hand.

There were times Scott was almost sorry for Snell. The guy simply could not cut it. Was punching way out of his class. They shook and Scott improvised something about Snell making a big deal himself someday.

"I hope." Snell looked miserable, then more so as he said, "Isn't it a shame about Patterson? Losing her like that."

"She wasn't a player, Snelly." Making it bluff and brash, projecting an image. "She didn't deserve to be here."

"All the same—"

"How many times, eh? It's not personal, it's biz-ey-neice." Scott gave the word an Italian spin, sounding like one of the Don's men in an old gangster movie.

"I just keep thinking..."

"You've got nothing to worry about," Scott told him, feeling generous. "Beaman will be lost long before you even have to start worrying." Scott looked out across the office. Maybe this is was what generals feel like, watching the front lines shift and change. Knowing one snafu could blitz the entire battle plan.

Still no sign of her.

"And Reardon, probably," he added, thinking: I'm not letting that rain on my parade.

All the same, he paused a moment as he headed back to his own desk, looking at her empty cubicle and wondering.

✶

Despite buzzing from Virtuex, Scott was careful not to appear to be slacking. He stayed late, then pushed to ensure as little downtime before the start of the next day as possible. Even subjectively, it seemed like he walked out of the office only to come straight back in again. Half an hour earlier than anyone else. Another point to him. As his colleagues rolled in, he was already hard at it.

It wasn't all for their benefit. New rules had recently been introduced following some scandal in another company. Now every keystroke and packet transmitted was logged and analysed by state-of-the-art AIs. Aside from sniffing out wrongdoing, what the AIs found influenced your bonus at the end of the month.

So Scott worked. But as he did so, his mind drifted. Somewhere, just beyond the horizon, was the next Virtuex. The big score that would push him further up the ranks. It had to be there. He knew it was.

Most of the morning passed in a blur. He was dimly aware of Temperley yelling, and an argument between a couple of Assistant Deps vying for the same promotion slot. There was a hush around 10:30, followed by a buzz of whispering which ramped-up enough to bring Temperley out of his office to give someone else a full-on basting. All of which barely registered with Scott.

The gossip around the coffee machine at eleven o'clock was all about Beaman. That hush a half-hour earlier had been caused by the man's sudden departure. His chronic under-performance had been no secret, but his loss caught everyone by surprise. Silently, Scott kicked himself for missing the show, especially after predicting it the day before.

Damn.

Heading back to his desk, he rechecked his tally. Solidly green, of course, but he couldn't afford to lose focus again. Not in a highly competitive environment like this. It was too easy to slip.

Which was why he couldn't help tinkering with the Patagonia project when he sat down again. He shouldn't, except after hours, but if he could just get a couple of subsidiary holdings to collateralize—

"Hear you had a minor success yesterday. Sorry I missed it."

Scott froze, fingers over the keyboard. Sorcha was looking at him over the top of his cubicle.

"They say every dog has his day." She smiled, slowly, as she said it.

"Why, thank you, Ms Reardon." With a casual flourish, Scott cleared the screen. From the angle she was standing, he reckoned Sorcha couldn't have seen anything. Sitting back, hands behind his head, he smiled, smug and challenging. "Coming from you, that's some compliment. I mean, you'd know all about dogs."

"Cheap shot, Scotty." She slapped the partition top, turning away. "Enjoy it while it lasts."

He opened his mouth but said nothing. Partly, he wondered if her parting shot counted against his day's tally. Mostly, Scott was trying to ignore the spear of lust transfixing him as he stood and watched Sorcha walk away.

★

There were two attempts to shoot him down in the team meeting next morning. The first, from Sorcha, was more a feint than anything.

Hardly worth the effort blocking and turning it back on her.

Temperley smiled at Scott just the same.

Maybe it was that smile that made him almost miss the second swipe. Temperley was an old player, after all, and having him onside made Scott feel safer. So it wasn't until Snell stumbled over a point he had failed to make already, that Scott saw just exactly what was up.

"It's amazing the number of companies in this position," Snell mumbled, red-faced at having everyone looking at him. "When the next quarterlies come in, I bet we see real fluctuations in the markets. Handoton and Transwestern are bound to go down, as is Cytain, Goldmarque–"

"Just a second–" Scott slammed his hand on the table. Cytain was one of Virtuex's main subsidiaries.

The argument made the meeting overrun by twenty minutes. By the end, Scott held his position. Even so, it was a close thing. The shock of an attack coming from Snell, of all people, almost robbed him of the ability to think. Afterwards, he stormed after Snell.

"You know I firmed up the Cytain issue before I made the deal."

"I'm sorry, Scott." Snell gave him this earnest, conflicted look. "But I really felt the point needed to be made. I mean, it's our duty–"

"Don't give me that crap. You think Temperley–"

"But, Scott, it was Temperley who told me to raise it at the meeting."

Scott could only stand, slack-jawed, as Snell walked away.

"What's the matter, Scotty?" Sorcha appeared beside him. "Never been savaged by a dead sheep before?"

She gave him that smile again. He couldn't help noticing the highlights sliding over the curve of her lips. How soft and red they looked.

"Snell? Snell's nothing." It wasn't Snell he was worried about.

"Maybe. All the same, Scotty, you should be careful who you choose to be friends with."

Sorcha gave Temperley's office a brief glance before walking slowly away. It took precious moments to tear his eyes away from her hips, the way her dress shaped itself around her buttocks.

Could Snell have done a deal with Temperley? Had the whole meeting been a setup?

His hands shook as he figured his score.

Not good. That loss of face (being sideswiped by Snell for Christ's sake!) had eaten deeply into the credit Virtuex had earned him. He needed to get ahead of all this. Really far ahead.

He needed Patagonia operational.

✱

Scott worked even harder over the next week. This time, however, the minimal downtime was all for his own benefit. He even stopped keeping a close score of those minor points of day-to-day one-upmanship he had once valued so highly. Now he was only interested in the project.

Things did not start well. Incredibly, despite the early hour, he arrived the first day to find someone already in Temperley's office. Former office.

Temperley was lost.

His replacement, Kosygin, turned out to be a hardcore berserker. Headhunted from a rival combine, he was fanatically ambitious and set on making his mark. Big changes, more productivity than Temperley ever managed. All the same, Kosygin seemed grudgingly impressed by Scott's early appearance. Previously, that would've been more kudos to his score. Now, he worried Kosygin would make it harder to get Patagonia operational.

When everyone had arrived, Kosygin gave a short speech setting out his agenda. No one appeared happy about the change. Snell definitely looked surprised to see Temperley gone.

It was small compensation. Confidence shaken, Scott found himself avoiding Snell. He could not even trust himself to fence with Sorcha. Feeling isolated, he tried not to clock-watch until finishing time.

Finally.

Luckily, not even Kosygin worked late. Scott, forgetting caution, attacked Patagonia with a vengeance.

What he was doing fell into a grey area. Strictly speaking, it was against the rules, although the rules were vague enough to leave wriggle room. That said, the supervisor AIs would ordinarily be all over him and Scott would probably be all over. It had taken an additional three months beyond the eight he'd spent planning the project to find exactly what he needed. Behind veils of anonymity, Scott hired a post-grad scriptjunkie at the Shanghai Institute of Advanced Computing to build him a ghost environment. Stored on a single memory stick, the environment piggybacked onto the company's system almost invisibly. What little did show through was so diffuse the AIs were unlikely to connect it all together before the next half-yearly log audit. By which time, it wouldn't matter.

Moving up his timetable, he worked frantically to pull together the remaining pieces. This deal wouldn't simply mean an astronomical bonus. It was a ticket straight to Permanent Management. Executive jet, luxury apartment, expensive women, expense account. It was the biggest score in corporate history.

He wasn't going to let it slip away.

★

"This guy is a real example to you all." Kosygin started clapping. Dutifully everyone else joined in. Scott worked on his smile. And clapped loudly.

Kosygin shook Snell's hand. Snell, blushing, thanked everybody and headed towards his new cubicle.

As the crowd drifted away, Scott noticed he was standing next to Sorcha.

"I see you're not looking so hot, Scotty." Her smile was unreadable. "Not working too hard, are you?"

"Not as hard as some." He nodded towards Snell. "Think he's being groomed for the top?"

"I like the sound of that. Being on top."

The silence grew taut between them. He struggled to appear cool, fighting the urge to lick his top lip. Nevertheless, Scott broke Sorcha's gaze first.

Back at his desk, he tried to concentrate. But the monitor screen faded as the morning replayed itself. That offhand crack about working too hard had hit too close. It was a given: the higher you climbed, the more of your ass you showed for people to poke spears at. If the strain of putting together Patagonia was becoming obvious, it made him even more vulnerable. And he was becoming vulnerable. Kosygin was pushing through his wholesale changes and slamming down on anyone not cutting it. With so little downtime, the extra fatigue was making it harder for Scott to do his legit work effectively. Little mistakes were mounting up, eating away at his credit.

Unless the project flew in the next couple of days, he'd be lost.

"Hmm, Scott, sorry to disturb but–"

Snell hesitated before sitting down beside Scott's desk. Scott jumped. Fighting to recover, he schmoozed Snell while trying not to appear obstructive as the other man asked a seemingly endless string of questions. By the time Snell left, Scott was exhausted. He slumped in his chair.

And only then noticed the ghost environment was still running on the monitor.

∗

It felt like it wouldn't take much more for it all to crash and burn.

Scott was convinced Snell was following an agenda. It was like he'd been wearing distorting goggles before. Scott couldn't understand how he had been conned by Snell's candyass act. He knew an operator when he saw one. It was obvious now, easy to translate everything Snell did into something he would do himself.

Snell was a player after all. A good one. Snell had guessed something. Time was running out.

With so little downtime, the fatigue weighting was making life harder each day. He tried to suck it up, push ahead. But he only had to look at the smile on Snell's face each morning – a smile that only twelve days ago had appeared so innocent – to see the threat.

"You need to slow down, Scotty."

She was watching him again over the top of the cubicle.

"Stop and you die." Mumbled this time, no passion behind it.

"I mean it. You'll burn out."

"Won't you be happy."

"Not… exactly."

Scott took a while to answer. "I guess I have been pushing hard."

"I like to push hard, too."

He didn't know how to read Sorcha's eyes.

"But not against an immovable object." She tilted her head towards the other side of the office. Snell's cubicle. "Luckily, most objects aren't immovable. Take care, Scotty."

∗

Scott told himself it was justified. Like the Don's men in that old gangster movie, defending their turf. Some things just had to be done.

He still didn't like it. The op was a deep charcoal grey tending firmly towards black, way beyond anything he'd done up to now.

With Patagonia still needing three more days to mature, though, he finally convinced himself he had to go forward with the plan. There was no other option.

At least, that's what Scott told himself.

Snell had kept up his act without a slip. The gormless smile, klutz manner. Mr Out-of-His-Depth. Scott watched for signs the other man was going to act on what he had seen on the monitor. But Snell apparently had other targets in mind. Coffee machine gossip maintained Snell's lucky streak was so hot, Sorcha would be the next to be lost. Snell was moving in on her like a smart missile.

Positioning a mirror in the corner of his desk in the hope of catching anyone trying to sneak up on him, he had checked and rechecked the ghost environment. The deal was shaping, gathering momentum. If Snell was really after Sorcha, he would be in the clear. There'd be no need for pre-emptive action.

But the clincher came when Kosygin carpeted Scott for being so sloppy. The dressing down came within minutes of Snell having had a long, private, heart-to-heart with Kosygin. In this world, coincidence never happened.

It turned out to be ridiculously easy. He had squirrelled away a few pieces of dirt over the last couple of years. Saving them for a rainy but never thinking he would ever deploy them. Using the ghost environment, there was nothing to slipping underneath the AIs and making it look as though someone had made a poor job of deleting evidence of a particularly nasty piece of malfeasance. Creating the breadcrumb trail took a little longer.

That much Scott could manage himself. The coup de grace came thanks to his pet scriptjunkie. Notionally, an AI's ability to self-reflect made it next to impossible to do what he was attempting to do without being noticed. Somehow or other, the scriptjunkie had found a way of fooling the company's monitoring systems into creating false memories. Each time the system re-examined itself, checking for errors, it simply reinforced the mistake. As far as the AIs were now concerned, those half-deleted files had always led back to Snell's personal dataspace.

It was all beyond Scott but, by the time he logged out that night, the hit had taken place.

✱

Snell was lost before close of business the following day.

Scott happened to be walking across the office at the time, Snell's cubicle dead ahead. One moment, Snell was sitting there looking bewildered. The next, no more Snell.

There was nothing to stop Patagonia now.

In the quiet after the office had emptied, he loaded the ghost environment and checked progress. All ripe and ready. He clapped his hands together.

"I like to see a man who enjoys his work."

Sorcha grinned at him from over the top of the partition.

"You look happy yourself." Casual, casual, Scott quit the ghost environment and sat back. Sorcha came around and sat on his desk beside him.

"Well why not? That horrid little pillock, Snell, got his today." She paused. Scott was painfully aware of how close she was. The sound of her hand stroking her knee, skirt hissing over stocking. Sorcha's perfume filled the cubicle.

"And I've got... you to thank, Scotty. Haven't I?"

He lunged forward. She met him halfway. Hands grasping, lips coming together hard. Scott tried to lift her from the desk. Sorcha leaned back, pulling him off balance a moment as she squirmed beneath him.

Then, panting, she pushed him off, slithering to her feet before grabbing him again. The chair flew back into the partition before careening out the cubicle.

They ended up in the ladies toilets, stall pressing close so there was little room. Sorcha tried to turn, make Scott sit on the pedestal. He resisted, hands and mouth moving practically by themselves while he kept her facing towards the cistern. While he remained standing.

On top.

Exhausted and happy, Scott allowed himself some downtime afterwards. It was only as the office dropped away that he realised he couldn't remember what had happened to the ghost environment's memory stick.

✱

Scott went back into the office the first second he could. He almost paused outside the cubicle, afraid of what he might find. But when he looked, the stick was still in his workstation. The only thing wrong was that he'd forgotten to shut down the workstation itself. A minor reprimand, nothing more. And, after today, completely unimportant.

The office was beginning to fill up, people appearing around the corner just beyond the coffee machine. He glanced at his watch. Ten minutes more and Patagonia would be set.

Too nervous to even pretend to work, Scott stood just outside his cubicle. Waiting. Across the room, Sorcha came in. Their eyes met. She gave him that smile of hers. Maybe he was fooling himself, but there seemed to be a flash of something in her expression. Something that looked like lust.

Mind racing with possibilities, Scott dropped into his chair. He had to see how things were going.

He launched the ghost environment. Its interface unfurled across the desktop.

And froze.

Walls of black light surrounded the cubicle, cutting Scott off from the rest of the office. Workstation, desk, the cubicle all vanished.

Knowing it was pointless, Scott still tried throwing his shoulder against the black cylinder now surrounding him. No sense of resistance, no rebound. He simply found himself standing, motionless again.

Text began to appear in the blackness. Red letters flashing ILLEGAL GAMEPLAY as a voice calmly explained that another player had brought Scott's activities to the Moderators' attention. Scott tried arguing, shouting at the top of his voice. It was no use.

He was lost.

★

Sid jerked upright on the mattress, tearing the skullcap from his head. There was a moment of disorientation when he expected to see the office, not his tiny fibreboard room. Then he slumped back and stared at the grimy ceiling. It must be late morning, judging from the stifling heat. The mattress squeaked, sagging springs suddenly all-too-familiar. With a groan, Sid turned over and groped until he found the skullcap.

It seemed okay. Making himself care, Sid looked over the console lying on the floor just above the head of the mattress. Modsticks hedge-hogged around its edges, screen smeared and scuffed. It must have passed through a dozen or more hands before Sid got hold of it. Even with all the mods, it was only just in-spec enough for him to take part at all.

Not that that mattered now.

He turned the console off, lodging it in the gap behind a loose board in the wall where, with any luck, nobody would find it and pinch it.

Someone was coming out of the communal lavs as he went in. No hellos, only a mumbled "They've cut the water ration again" as the woman scuffed away down the corridor. Sid grunted, used the chemical toilet, and stood in front of the row of chipped hand basins. Brown spots covered the mirror like smallpox. The reflection behind the blemishes was disappointing. Scott had been well-muscled and low-key handsome. Sid was skinny and hollow-eyed through not eating enough. He didn't like this version at all.

It was nearly noon when he left the block. The streets teemed in the fierce sunlight, three dozen different nationalities hustling and pushing, three dozen languages all bellowed at top volume. Instinctively, Sid dodged bicycles and rickshaws as they themselves weaved between gaping potholes and lumbering electric lorries. A new shantysquat sprawled out of a long-derelict office block and up the pavement like a fungus, throwing out mycelium of rancid burlap and fibreboard. Still running on automatic, Sid ignored its ragged tenants, brushing past outstretched hands or sidestepping when one of them tried to hold him up. The stench from the blocked gutters hardly registered. Instead, all he thought about was the office. And Sorcha.

Grudgingly, he had to admit she'd played him wonderfully. Sorcha must have lifted the memory stick before they'd stumbled into the toilets and put it back after he'd entered downtime. To be as realistic and immersive as possible, the environment had a certain flexibility built into it. Contact with players in parallel environments – like scriptjunkies – even a little rule bending: these things were tolerated, if not officially sanctioned aspects of gameplay. The trick was primarily not getting found out, at least not until after you achieved Permanent Management status.

Today's queue for food tokens wound for hundreds of metres up the street from the civic centre. Luckily, Sid had collected his during that final chunk of downtime. There was still a wait of an hour before the gaunt, harassed man at the serving hatch finally exchanged Sid's token for a small, vacuum-sealed package.

"Ration's cut again," the man grunted in reply to Sid's expression.

Without much hope, Sid checked the bulletin board. Not a hint of a job in baselife. Apparently, according to the AI handling his case, there wasn't even chance of being conscripted to work on the big flood defence programme down south. The project was already mob-handed.

To add to the happiness of the day, his case handler finished by warning Sid all benefits were being cut again from the first of next month.

Before leaving, he glanced through his personal messagespace. One post, forwarded from his gaming account:

"It's how the game goes. No hard feelings. Thinking of you from the lofty heights of Permanent Management, Sorcha."

Sid idly wondered who Sorcha really was. Maybe she was management in baselife, just as she now was in gamelife. Much more probably, she lived in a place something like this. Dodging a donkey cart, he crossed the road. The civic centre stood on a low hill, giving a view over the fallows towards the heart of the city. It was like looking at a mountainscape: ridge-lines of concrete and graphene rising higher the closer they were to the centre, where they formed needle-sharp pinnacles snagging the few clouds in an otherwise empty sky. Being kilometres away did nothing to make those towers look any smaller.

In gamelife he had seen them up close. Been inside them. In baselife, Sid had never visited the centre of the city. Could not even afford the toll to pass into the inner suburbs.

All he wanted was to look from ground level, to have to crane back and still not be able to see their tops.

Getting caught pulling a fast one usually meant your tally being zeroed and starting again at the bottom, say as an intern janitor. But two major grey-area plays like this meant permanent expulsion. Sorcha had known that. She'd seen how much Scott/Sid had needed to get to the top and used it against him.

He still couldn't honestly blame her. It was just biz-ey-neice after all.

Sid turned away, taking in the food queue, the potholes, the shabby buildings retrofitted with low-grade greentech.

To look at those towers close-up just once in baselife. If only that was possible.

There was no thought. He simply started walking. Figuring odds, checklisting. A phantom baselife presence good enough to fool the office moderators, longun scriptjunkie to pull it together. Scraping up the payment. Pilfering enough electricity to keep the console going. Maybe even squeezing in some extra mods. Whatever it took. Anything. Anything to keep playing the game.

AFTERGAME

By Jason D Wittman

The world was a square of stone.

It lay there, beneath the glowing sun and the shining moon, a vast square of marble, divided into sixty-four smaller squares, half of pearl, half of smoky blue. This geometric construction comprised the known world in its entirety; beyond lay only black desert, and the horizon.

And this world, like others, had its inhabitants.

King Cyrus of House Ivory advanced diagonally forward to Queen's Knight Six to capture the pawn that checked him. With practiced ease he threw one of his needles, which spun in a tight arc and sunk a quarter-inch into the pawn's neck.

The convulsions took hold before she could even start screaming. Cyrus watched her as she fell, savored her spasms, before he kicked her body aside to take her place on the square.

"Medics!" he bellowed. "Attend to the Queen!"

From the Southeastern Keep on Queen Five, a thousand tiny clockwork automatons flew on golden filament wings, over bodies and blood and rusted armor, toward Queen Alexandra Sicklefist of House Ivory.

She stood, an imposing figure in bright raiment, her armor like white enamel, her skirt of silver mail, on Queen's Rook Four. Coppery hair cascaded to her waist. Where her hands should have been were instead a pair of wicked steel sickles. A mask in the form of an expressionless white face hid her features. She had survived many battles – most recently she had brought the Northeastern Keep to ruin – but now she was wounded in several places, and she favored one leg. King Cyrus dispatched the medical automatons because he wanted her healthy, especially now that the war was about to end.

But when the automatons reached Alexandra, she refused them. Instead, speaking softly to the tiny mechanisms, she pointed one sickle toward the still-convulsing pawn.

And in obedience, the automatons went there.

"What are you doing!?" Cyrus demanded.

But Alexandra ignored him as the automatons settled on the pawn and, through hundreds of pinprick injections, ended her suffering forever. The pawn's spasms subsided, her body stilled.

"Idiot!" said Cyrus. "She was already as good as dead! I sent the automatons for you!"

Without a glance at Cyrus, Alexandra said, "She did us no dishonor. She deserved a better death than you gave her."

"That does not entitle you–!"

"Sire!" called Bishop Malachi from where he stood on Queen's Bishop Seven. "This act is not worth your anger. You will win the war easily regardless."

"But that still doesn't–!"

"You can win the war just as easily without her." With one hand, Malachi pointed to the Keep on Queen Five. "There will be plenty of time to settle this matter once we have won the war."

Cyrus, placated, fell silent.

Indifferent to his anger, Alexandra turned to the Queen of House Sable.

"What was the soldier's name?" she asked.

"Jane," Queen Jacqueline of House Sable replied, conveying thanks through her gaze.

"Jane," Alexandra repeated, then turned to the pawn's silent corpse. She raised her right sickle hand in salute, and remained that way for a score of heartbeats. Then she dropped her salute, and turned forward to face King Melchior standing four stones away.

✳

On Queen's Rook One, King Melchior of House Sable knew he was doomed. Alexandra threatened him from King's Rook Five, the Southeastern Keep from Queen Four, and none of his options led anywhere. But because the war was not ended, Melchior had to make a move. A choice between dooms.

"Melchior," Jacqueline called to him from Queen One.

He looked to her. "Yes, love?"

Queen Jacqueline Hookhand wore the hue of her allegiance, blackened plates and a high collar protecting her torso and neck, a wide skirt of boiled leather reaching to the ground. Her close-cropped hair shone also black, as did her left eye. A patch covered her right socket. A hook had replaced her left hand.

She indicated the Queen of House Ivory.

"Let me take her."

Melchior considered. It was a useless move, a spiteful blow before dying. But so was every other.

With a nod, Melchior granted assent.

✱

Jacqueline strode toward Alexandra, drawing her sword. Alexandra readied her own weapons.

Jacqueline stopped. They regarded each other, facing a fight only one would survive. Jacqueline sensed the pride in Alexandra, and the bitterness of wounded pride.

Softly, Jacqueline asked. "Do you yield?"

Alexandra stood dumbfounded. It was a moment before she found the presence of mind to say, "What?"

"Do you yield?" Jacqueline repeated. "Do you want to live?"

Alexandra frowned within her mask. Such a thing was within the rules. But it had never been done before.

"Do you want to live?" Jacqueline said again.

With the question phrased thus, the answer was obvious. "Yes."

"Then go in there." Jacqueline pointed to the Northwestern Keep on King's Bishop Six. "You will be freed when this is over."

"Jacqueline," called Melchior, equally thunderstruck. "What are you doing?"

"This is not betrayal, my love," Jacqueline replied with a gentle gaze. "I merely give thought to the future."

Alexandra looked at her. "What future is that?"

Jacqueline only said, "Later. Go."

"Oh, just go and be done with it," said King Cyrus. "Why look a gift horse in the mouth?"

Alexandra's jaw clenched. She turned, limped to the Northwestern Keep, and went inside. The gate slammed to with frightening vehemence.

With Alexandra's capture completed, it was now House Ivory's move. But Cyrus hesitated, as puzzled by Jacqueline's actions as anyone.

Looking to Bishop Malachi, he asked, "What happened there?"

"It is hard to say, my king," the Bishop replied. His left thumb rubbed the scars where two fingers had been. "But it was all legal and above board. And Melchior is yours for the mating. Kill him, you have one less problem to deal with."

Cyrus nodded. "You're right. Why postpone the inevitable?" He called out: "Southeastern Keep to Queen Eight!" He beamed at Melchior. "Checkmate!"

The marble fortress made its ponderous way to the northern edge, and stopped. Then, having achieved checkmate, it floated westward, toward Melchior.

The King of House Sable chose not to watch death approaching. Instead, he looked to his wife, who held his gaze, caressed him with her eyes. King Cyrus looked on with delight. Malachi clasped his hands in prayer.

A pawn of House Sable stood on King's Knight Five, veteran of many battles, his beard streaked with white where scars lay beneath, his ears no less notched than his sword. His name was Simon. He stood at attention, feeling he should bear witness to his king's demise.

The death was quick, though unpleasant to watch.

"And now," said King Cyrus, turning to Jacqueline, "we will discuss your surrender."

Jacqueline did not reply. After a moment, she started walking in Cyrus' direction, sword still unsheathed. Fearing the worst, Cyrus readied his needles. But she ignored him, and strode on to the Southeastern Keep.

"What are you doing?" Cyrus cried. "Come back here!"

Jacqueline did not respond. When she reached the Southeastern Keep, she swung her blade and destroyed it.

Cyrus reddened. "How dare you? I am the victor here, by right and rule!"

Jacqueline looked on the wreckage with a vague smile.

"The war is over," she said. "The rules no longer apply."

Spinning on her heel, she went off in another direction.

"Where are you going?" Cyrus shouted.

Jacqueline entered the Northwestern Keep, slamming the gates behind her.

"What the hell does she think she's doing?" Cyrus demanded. "I win the war, fairly and uncontestably, and everyone ignores me!"

He pointed at Simon. "You there! Go into that Keep and tell Queen Jacqueline that I demand to see her immediately!"

Simon hesitated. Victorious or not, Cyrus was not his king. But after a moment, he obliged. He was curious himself about Queen Jacqueline's intentions.

II: PAWN AND QUEENS

Simon entered the fortress. The gates closed behind him, and echoes reverberated down the corridor.

Time and space did not behave within the Keeps as they did without. Seen from outside, the Keeps were simple monoliths, a good deal shorter than the Kings and Queens. Seen from inside, however, the Keeps were... larger.

Simon paused in the airy coolness of the Keep interior, looking up at lanterns flickering from rafters high above.

"Where is Her Majesty?" he asked.

"She went that way," the gatekeeper replied. It was a clockwork automaton, a torso, head, and arms permanently affixed to the masonry – a machine that followed instructions. "To the dungeons."

Simon made way down the corridor.

*

At about the same time, Jacqueline entered the dungeons.

On reaching the foot of the dungeon stairwell, she stopped, leaned her forehead against the wall, and wept for Melchior.

Salt tears fell on the floorstones, for Melchior, for Bishop Jacopus, for Sir Robert, for all the dead. Houses Ivory and Sable had waged this war since time began. And now that the war was over... what? Queen Jacqueline Hookhand wept in no small part because she knew no answer to that question. She did not know what all these deaths had purchased.

But she had come here to find an answer. When her tears were spent, she composed herself and resumed her way.

At regular intervals along the corridor, more clockwork automatons sat moored, both guards and keymasters. They straightened to attention as Jacqueline passed by, until she arrived at Alexandra's cell.

"Has she said anything?" Jacqueline asked of the automaton before her.

"No," it replied.

"The door is locked?"

"Yes, as per dungeon protocol."

"Unlock it. She won't try to escape."

As the automaton obeyed, a metallic rattling emanated from up the corridor. Turning, Jacqueline saw another automaton, a head, arms, and chest attached to a low wagon. Inside the wagon were various bottles and bandages.

"The prisoner was injured," said the first automaton. "As per dungeon protocol, a medical automaton was summoned."

"Of course." Reaching into the wagon, Jacqueline picked up the bottles and bandages. "All the same, I think I shall tend her wounds. There are things I would discuss with her."

"Yes, Majesty."

And it opened the door.

Jacqueline saw Alexandra only as a dim blur in the darkness. Among the medical supplies were a candle, and matches. Jacqueline used these to illuminate the cell.

Alexandra sat in a far corner, still wearing those sickles, and the mask.

"So," she said. "The war is over."

Jacqueline nodded. "Yes."

Alexandra sighed. "I am sorry. Your husband fought well."

"Yes. Thank you."

Silence.

Alexandra seemed to squint beneath her mask.

"And now that it's over," she said, "what now? You seem to have… ideas."

Jacqueline indicated the salves and gauze. "I thought we might discuss that while I tended your wounds."

Alexandra tilted her head to one side.

"First," She held up her arms, "would you help me out of these sickles?"

It took time – there was only one hand between them – but eventually they removed the right-hand blade. It revealed a simple stump, long since healed over.

Removing the second blade revealed a whole and healthy hand.

There was a grin in Alexandra's voice: "I lost the right hand early on – against Sir Robert, remember? – and when our automatons fitted me for the sickle, I said, 'Make another for the left arm. They'll think I amputated them both.'" The automatons worked at blinding speed, so the enemy would not see what was done. "Rumor spread like wildfire, didn't it?"

Jacqueline laughed softly. "I think you're intimidating enough, Sicklefist, without…"

She trailed off as her gaze fell on the mask.

When she raised her hand to remove it, Alexandra made no move to stop her.

There was only a long scar slashing across her right eye. The eye itself was askew, its pupil a gaping hole in a sea of white; the lids would not close properly. The other eye blinked at Jacqueline, an iris of metallic blue beneath an elegant coppery eyebrow.

Alexandra gestured with her stump. "Another deception."

"It's a shame," said Jacqueline. "Your other eye is beautiful."

Alexandra said nothing.

"We'd best see to those wounds," Jacqueline said.

Alexandra grimaced as she tested her limbs. "I've been stiffening ever since I got here."

"I am sorry." Opening a bottle of ointment, Jacqueline applied it to a cut. "I should have told the automatons to assign you better quarters."

"I should have asked for them." Alexandra shrugged. "These wounds will heal, one way or another. When I came here, I…"

She stopped.

"I…needed to be alone more than anything."

After a silence, Jacqueline ventured to speak.

"The best way to know someone is to fight them," she said. "You and I have fought since time began. And I have come to… one conclusion, among others."

She phrased her next words delicately.

"You don't… approve of King Cyrus."

Alexandra's fist clenched. She ground her teeth.

"*Needles*," she hissed. "Poisoned needles are the weapons of a coward."

Jacqueline nodded.

Alexandra went on. "And he sacrifices his men as if they were… were…" She shook her head. "He demands absolute loyalty and gives none in return! Their integrity was repaid with death!"

"He would probably argue," said Jacqueline, "that that was how he won."

"So do you want someone like that to rule?!?"

The automaton in the corridor peered apprehensively into the cell.

"It would seem," said Jacqueline, "that you do not."

Alexandra looked away. Eventually, a tear descended from her eye.

"I am ashamed to have served him," said the Queen of House Ivory.

Jacqueline put a hand on her arm.

"There is something you should know," she said. "Before coming here, I destroyed the Southeastern Keep." She paused. "I hope you do not object?"

Alexandra shrugged. "Just a pile of stone. What of it?"

"Well, without the Keep – and without you – King Cyrus only has Bishop Malachi to fight for him. House Sable, on the other hand, still has one Pawn, this Keep, and myself."

She held out her hand to Alexandra.

"And if you and I joined forces…"

Alexandra looked at the hand, stunned.

"Majesty?"

Jacqueline turned to see a pawn standing at the door.

"Yes, Simon?"

"Begging your pardon, Majesty, but… what are we going to do? King Cyrus awaits our surrender. If he waits too much longer, he might decide to destroy this Keep, as you destroyed his…"

"I wouldn't put it past him," said Alexandra.

"…and I wouldn't be able to defend the keep by myself…"

Jacqueline nodded. "Of course not, Simon. But consider the situation." She paused for emphasis. "This Keep currently rests on a light square. Bishop Malachi patrols the dark squares. We should have plenty of time to execute my plan."

"Plan?" Simon blinked, confused. "Majesty… the war is over–"

"That simply means the rules have changed," said Jacqueline. "Simon, listen to me." She rose, stepped close to the pawn and spoke gently. "This war was fought according to the laws of Nature, and according to those laws, Cyrus won. But what did he win? Can you tell me that?"

Simon said nothing.

"All this war proved," Jacqueline went on, "is that Cyrus is more cunning and ruthless than was Melchior. But I think it also proved that Cyrus is severely lacking in foresight. He gave no thought to anything beyond the end of the war. I plan to take advantage of that."

After a moment, Simon asked. "What would you have me do?"

"Leave the Keep," said Jacqueline, "and make for the southern border. If you can achieve promotion, that would give us a significant advantage."

Simon bowed. "It shall be done, Majesty," he said, and left.

Jacqueline turned back to Alexandra. "And what of your decision?"

"Join forces?" Alexandra queried. "Can we even do that?"

"You want to."

Alexandra nodded, admitting it.

"I would have Malachi spared," she said. "He has a sense of honor."

"Can you convince him to join us?"

"I believe so."

"Agreed, then."

Jacqueline resumed work on the injuries. When she finished, she rose and offered her hand again.

Alexandra had only her left hand, Jacqueline only her right. There was some awkwardness, but finally they clasped hands, and Jacqueline pulled Alexandra to her feet.

III: BISHOP/KNIGHT

"Where the devil is that girl?" Cyrus asked. The pawn showed no more sign of reappearing than Jacqueline.

"Before she left, sire," said Malachi, "Queen Jacqueline said, 'The war is over. The rules no longer apply.' Perhaps she is trying to determine what to do next."

"There is nothing else to do!" Cyrus shouted. "Beyond the end of the war, there is nothing else except subservience to the victor!" He threw up his hands. "Does she think I went through the trouble of winning this war just so I could stand here waiting for her?"

"Understand, sire," Malachi ventured, "that I am only trying to guess her mind." He looked to the pile of rubble that had been the Southeastern Keep. "She captured Queen Alexandra alive, and sent her to the Northwestern Keep. So you were already minus your Queen. Then she destroyed the Southeastern Keep, depriving you of its power as well. So she has another Queen, a Keep, and a Pawn, whereas you have only..."

His heart sank.

"...me."

"Another Queen?" Cyrus queried. "You mean Alexandra? She would never betray us!"

Malachi gaped. Surely Cyrus could not be ignorant of Alexandra's contempt for him?

"She is House Ivory!" Cyrus yelled. "She always will be! Those are the Rules! They don't change just because the war is over, or someone chooses to ignore them! Look at this!" He walked over and kicked the corpse of a horse from House Sable. Its only response was that of dead flesh. "The Dead remain Dead! And I doubt that Jacqueline could will it otherwise!"

"I don't understand it entirely myself, sire. But Jacqueline clearly thinks she can do something. How else do you explain her actions?"

Just then, the pawn emerged from the Northwestern Keep.

"Well?" Cyrus called out. "Where is she?"

The pawn said, "Her Majesty Queen Jacqueline has instructed me to set out for the southern border."

He turned, and began walking.

Cyrus grew livid. "How dare he! They can't–!"

"Sire." Malachi pointed to the Keep. "Look."

There, atop the battlements, emerged Jacqueline and Alexandra, both in miniature. They watched Simon as he marched southward.

"Sire," said Malachi, "I was right. If that pawn promotes, the Queens won't even need to join the battle!"

Cyrus paled as the full reality of it finally dawned on him.

"We'll… we'll destroy the Keep, as they did ours! Both Queens will die in one stroke!"

"Begging your pardon, sire, but that's impossible. The light squares are beyond my reach, and the Keep rests on a light square! It can evade capture indefinitely! Jacqueline knows this! Sire," Malachi said, his face ashen, "we are lost."

This was not what Cyrus wanted to hear. He turned to the horse-carcass and kicked it again and again –

Then he stopped.

Cyrus stared at the carcass, wide-eyed.

"Yes," he murmured. "Why not? If she will not abide by the rules, why should I?"

Malachi frowned. "Sire?"

Cyrus looked across the battlefield. "What is that pawn doing now?"

Malachi turned to look. But before he could respond, he felt a sharp pain at the base of his skull.

Even as he cried out, his sight began dimming. Sinking to the ground, he turned to Cyrus, and saw the needle in his hand.

"It's only a sedative," Cyrus assured him. "When you awaken, those light squares will be within your reach…"

Malachi's last vision was of Cyrus picking up an abandoned dagger from the ground, turning to the horse's carcass, and slicing it open.

★

"Is your plan to let Simon do this by himself?" Alexandra asked. From the battlements, she watched the pawn make his slow way southward.

"I would accept such an outcome," Jacqueline replied. "But I am not counting on it. Cyrus sees the situation as well as we do. He knows he will have to do something. And when he does, we will react accordingly."

Alexandra nodded. "I just thought you might have sent Simon on that mission to restore his sense of purpose. He seemed… confused when he spoke. Lost, I would say."

"I noticed that," Jacqueline replied. "Since time began, the war was his life, his reason for being. In that he is not unique. I think that is why House Sable fought on, even when the outcome was no longer in question." She looked toward Simon. "Better to have an unachievable purpose than no purpose at all."

Alexandra looked away.

"Far worse to have a purpose you don't want to achieve."

"You no longer serve that purpose," Jacqueline said. "That was why I spared you."

Alexandra returned Jacqueline's gaze. "And I have not properly thanked you for it. I am grateful, Jacqueline."

Queen Jacqueline Hookhand gave her a gentle smile.

"So," said Alexandra. "Our purpose now is to bring down Cyrus – but what then? After that purpose is achieved, what is left?"

"You are right," said Jacqueline. "Any purpose, once achieved, dies in the achieving." She sighed. "We will, of course, give more thought to this once Cyrus is gone. But I thought it might be of interest to explore beyond this battlefield." She gestured to the black dunes beyond the borders. "See if there is anything out there beside desert."

Alexandra scanned the horizon, trying to find some landmark, something of interest –

When she looked northwest, she saw King Cyrus.

"What is he doing?"

Jacqueline looked.

Bishop Malachi had fallen. Kneeling over him with a knife, Cyrus had severed the Bishop's torso from his legs, and now he... yes, he was sewing the torso to the headless remains of a horse.

"It's clear what he's trying to do," said Jacqueline.

"Will it work?"

"Why give him the chance?"

Together, the queens left the battlements.

★

Cyrus worked quickly. If Malachi recovered too soon, it would complicate the operation.

The stitches were crude. The scar tissue would be hideous when healed. But the fruits of victory that Cyrus had rightfully earned were in jeopardy, and he would use all means necessary to keep them.

Finally, the work was finished. Cyrus examined it, looking to see if every knot would hold. As he did so, Malachi awakened.

"Get up," Cyrus said. "Look at yourself."

Not knowing what else to do, Malachi obeyed. He found it difficult – there were more legs than there were supposed to be, and they did not feel right.

"Come on!" Cyrus snapped. "Part of you must remember what it is to be a horse!"

At that, the part that had been a horse took charge. It lifted itself off the ground, standing on iron-shod hoofs. The part that had been Bishop Malachi flailed, making frightened, incoherent noises until the jostling stopped. He faced King Cyrus, wide-eyed, open-mouthed, trembling.

"There," said Cyrus, nodding. "Now the entire battlefield is within your reach." He pointed southeast. "Your mission is to slay that pawn before it reaches the southern border. Go."

Not knowing what else to do, Malachi obeyed.

Cyrus watched him go. If all went well, the King might try further experiments. It would, for instance, be a shame to let Malachi's legs go to waste...

★

Simon made steady progress. He had only King Cyrus and Bishop Malachi to worry about. Simon would be safe from Malachi as long as he stayed on the light stones, and he could easily outrun Cyrus. Promotion was all but his.

He looked back toward Cyrus and Malachi, to be certain before he made his next move. Then he saw that Bishop Malachi had fallen. Simon froze, wondering whether to take immediate advantage, or wait to see if this was a trick.

His orders were to make for the southern border. So that is what he did. For without orders, without purpose, what was he?

But after reaching the next stone, Simon turned back for a second look. Malachi's fall was clearly Cyrus' doing, and the king did not do such things on a whim.

King Cyrus had bisected Malachi through the waist. Then he had severed the head from a nearby horse.

When Cyrus began sewing them together, Simon took off at a dead run.

But it was too late. Before Simon could reach the border, Malachi cut him off.

Simon drew his sword and stared horrified at the aberration before him. The combined abilities of a Bishop and a Knight against a simple Pawn – this would be a complex dance at best.

Simon risked a glance toward the Northwestern Keep to see if Queen Jacqueline had seen. But she was not visible on the battlements.

Simon assumed a defensive posture. The creature moved to a different stone. It raised its iron-shod fore-hoofs; Malachi's hands swung a Bishop's staff...

But the creature seemed to fight itself as much as Simon. The two halves of its nature, being of different Houses, pursued different purposes. The horse's body reared, trying to shake off Malachi's torso. Its throes became so violent that blood began to trickle from the surgical stitches.

Eventually, Simon no longer felt in danger. He lowered his sword. He watched as the Malachi-creature stumbled, then fell to the ground, writhing in agony.

"Help me!" it screamed. The voice was Malachi's, though he might have been speaking for both halves. "I am torn! Part of me remembers you as a comrade! The other is under orders to slay you!" He put his hands to his ears, trying to silence the cacophony in his own skull. "Please help me! Even if it's by slaying me!"

Simon raised his sword, but tentatively. He pitied Malachi, and would have granted his wish. But he could not help thinking there might be another way.

Then it occurred to him.

Lowering his sword, he said, "Malachi... who did this to you?"

Through his anguish, Malachi managed to get out: "King... Cyrus!"

Simon stepped closer, brought his face close to Malachi's.

And he said, "How then do you owe him your loyalty?"

Malachi stopped struggling. His body went limp, but he still breathed, and for a long moment he lay there, his mind focused on Simon's words.

Finally, he got up. There was no duality of purpose now; all parts of the creature moved as one. He faced Simon, as one soldier to another, and saluted him.

"Thank you," Malachi said. Then he turned and sped toward Cyrus.

Simon watched him go. He himself could not go in that direction.

Not yet.

✱

The queens emerged from the Northwestern Keep to see Malachi approaching at full speed. Fearing the worst, Alexandra stepped in front of Jacqueline and raised her sickles.

"You have nothing to fear from me," said Malachi, slowing to a stop. "I know who my enemy is." He bowed to the Queen of House Ivory. "You have ever had my allegiance, Majesty. You were always loyal to your people."

Alexandra lowered her sickles.

"Together," said Jacqueline, "the three of us should be more than enough. Shall we go, then?"

"Yes," said Alexandra.

✱

From where he stood on King Seven, Simon watched Malachi join forces with the Queens. Then the three of them set out toward Cyrus.

This would soon be over. And Simon's presence was not required.

Since time began, the war had been his life, his purpose. Now that even this second war was ended, what purpose was left? Not just for himself, but for all remaining in this world?

Was there nothing they could – ?

Simon turned his gaze southward.

Queen Jacqueline's orders were for him to reach the southern border, and achieve promotion. Simon had yet to do that.

If, in carrying out those orders, he gave her something unexpected...

He took the final step, and arrived on King Eight.

IV: ROOK

Cyrus saw them coming, and knew he was doomed. But he would not go quietly. If he had any chance of surviving, it would not be by doing nothing. He would live forever, or die in the attempt.

In a concerted advance, Jacqueline Hookhand, Alexandra Sicklefist, and Malachi bore down on the King of House Ivory. Alexandra tore open his left sleeve with a flick of her sickle, and two score needles fell to the ground.

Deprived of his weapon of choice, King Cyrus resorted to a sword plucked from the battlefield. He fought well, it had to be said. He served the cause of his own preservation with as much passion and dedication as he expected others to.

But with two Queens and a Bishop-Knight hybrid as opponents, the outcome was all but inevitable. Presented with an opening, Malachi landed a kick to the jaw, and before Cyrus could recover, Jacqueline impaled him with her sword. Alexandra brought both sickles forward in a scissors motion, severing his head from his neck.

There followed an immense, empty silence.

Breathing deeply, Alexandra looked around, first at Malachi, then at Jacqueline.

"It is over," she said. "Finished."

Malachi gazed at the corpse, this final addition to the carrion strewn about the battlefield.

Jacqueline turned to him. "We are grateful for your assistance, Malachi – especially considering what you have gone through."

"You have your Simon to thank for that," Malachi replied. "He could have slain me – I had begged him to. Instead, he made me understand who my true enemy was."

Jacqueline smiled. "Then this victory is Simon's as much as ours."

She looked to the south, searching for Simon –

Then her hands leapt to her mouth, and she screamed.

Alexandra and Malachi followed her gaze. A dark granite Keep stood on King Eight where Simon had been. He had stepped to the edge, and promoted himself.

Jacqueline ran, ran all the way to the castle, as if through sheer speed she might bring Simon back. When she reached it, she placed her hands on the lifeless masonry, calling out Simon's name.

By the time Malachi and Alexandra joined her, she had already shed many tears.

Alexandra gathered Jacqueline into her arms, letting her weep on her shoulder.

"He was lost," Alexandra said. "He saw no purpose beyond this end. As you yourself said, the war was his life."

"But I told him!" Jacqueline protested. "The end of the war simply meant a change in the rules! With Cyrus gone, we would have been free to explore! To search for a purpose!" She tried to swallow against a constricted throat. "I told him…"

"Majesties," said Malachi. "The gate is opening."

They looked up to see the heavy iron door swing open. Intrigued despite their grief, they stepped up to look inside.

Just within the gate, moored in granite, sat another clockwork automaton. It looked just enough like Simon to make Jacqueline weep anew.

Seeing the newcomers, the automaton pointed further within the castle and said, "This way."

Following the gesture, they caught sight of… something… but it was too bright outside for them to see. So they stepped over the threshold, and inside.

Now they saw it with perfect clarity. For a long while they stood and stared in absolute silence, bathed in a warm white glow.

At last, Alexandra turned to her companions.

"Shall we?"

Malachi, mute in his amazement, nodded.

Jacqueline stared, hardly breathing as the tears of her grief dried away.

"Is this why you did it, Simon?" she whispered.

"Come," said Alexandra.

And the gate closed behind them as they went forward, out of this story, and into another.

BIOGRAPHIES

JP Alders
JP Alders is an Yorkshire exile currently residing in Derbyshire. When not attempting to write short stories he can be found attempting to get his moanings about modern life printed in the local paper for free. Other interests include Flapjacks.

Allen Ashley
Allen Ashley is an award-winning editor and a prize-winning author and poet. His latest book is as editor of "Astrologica: Stories of the Zodiac" (Alchemy Press, 2013). He works as a critical reader and a writing tutor, with several groups running across north London including Clockhouse London Writers. He was the sole judge for the British Fantasy Society Short Story Competitions in 2012 and 2013. Check out www.allenashley.com

Gary Budgen
Gary Budgen grew up and lives in London. He has had about twenty or so stories published in magazines and short story anthologies including *Interzone*, *Dark Horizons* and the *Where Are We Going* anthology from Eibonvale press. Recent work has appeared in *Sein und Werden*, *The Urban Green Man* anthology and *Theaker's Quarterly*. He is a member of Clockhouse London Writers. He can be found at http://garybudgen.wordpress.com/

Adam Craig
Adam's been writing seriously for only six years and so finds the experience of having to talk about himself in the third person, erm... rather odd. He's interested in books and film and music, all of which find their way into his writing one way or another. By the time you read this it's likely Adam will have had stories published by Alchemy and Dog Horn and (he really, really hopes) finished the novel he's currently working on. Feel free to contact Adam at: adamcraigsmail@gmail.com

Charlie Fish

Charlie Fish is a popular short story writer and screenwriter. His short stories have been published in several countries and inspired dozens of short film adaptations. Since 1996, he has edited www.fictionontheweb.co.uk, the longest-running short story site on the web. He was born in Mount Kisco, New York in 1980; and now lives in Brixton, south London with his wife and daughters. You can contact him at charlie@fictionontheweb.co.uk, and you can follow him on Twitter@ fishcharlie.

Beau Johnson

Beau Johnson lives up der in Canada with his wife and three boys. They are an unruly lot, the lot of them, but he loves them all the same. Especially his favorite, whom shall remain nameless (you know who you are). Ohters stories of Beau's can found in certain places across the Internet. Such places might include Undergound Voices, Shotgun Honey, Out Of The Gutter Online and/or Bartleby Snopes. He has paid them all to say nice things about him.

Natalie Perry

Natalie is happiest when she has a beautiful blank piece of freshly stretched paper, with an idea in her head and a pencil in her hand with her inks and watercolours waiting to pounce! Similarly, a pen in hand and and lined paper... ooooh, crisp lines paper for scribbling story ideas, makes her pretty cheery too. Other things that make Natalie happy are; her whole family being in one place at the same time, her wonderful husband, beautiful new baby and happy chickens and their fluffy bottoms, real vanilla ice cream with honey on, movie montages and sitting in the sun, or the snow, or the rain, with friends.

Diotima Sophia

Although not the original Diotima, the author does agree that the western world has invested far too much energy into separating the inseparable duo of mind and heart. Diotima has written widely on a number of subjects, including essays, fiction and poetry. Two of her latest books have been published by the Bibliotheca Alexandrina: Dancing God – a collection of poetry, and Goat Foot God, an examination of the Great God Pan; both available through Neos Alexandria (http://www. neosalexandria.org/publishing.htm). Her latest work of fiction is Tales in Vein, a series of short stories available in ebook and audio book format from Amazon. Her website can be found at: http://diotima-sophia.com/.

David Turnbull

David Turnbull is the author of a children's fantasy novel featuring dragon hunters and airships – *The Tale of Euan Redcap*. His short fiction has appeared in numerous magazines and anthologies, both online and in print. His most recent magazine publication was in *Lissette's Tales of the Imagination*. Recent anthologies include *Dandelions of Mars*, the Whortleberry Press tribute to Ray Bradbury and the forthcoming *Black Apples* anthology due for release shortly by Belladonna Press – as well as the forthcoming *Astrologica* anthology on *Alchemy Press*. He is member of Clockhouse London Writers.

Sandra Unerman

Sandra Unerman is a retired Government lawyer who lives in London. She has written fantasy for many years and has had stories published in Scheherazade and All Hallows magazines. She has recently graduated with an MA in Creative Writing from Middlesex University and she is a member of the London Clockhouse writers' group.

Jay Wilburn
Jay Wilburn left teaching after sixteen years to be a full time writer. He lives in the swamps of coastal South Carolina with his wife and two sons. Wilburn has published many horror and speculative fiction stories including his novels LOOSE ENDS and TIME EATERS. He has a piece in BEST HORROR OF THE YEAR volume 5. Wilburn is a featured author on the Dark and Bookish authors tour and documentary. Follow his many dark thoughts at JayWilburn.com and @AmongTheZombies on Twitter.

Jason D. Wittman
Jason D. Wittman lives and works in Minnesota. In addition to his fiction, he has two games (including a 6-player chess variant) published by Steve Jackson Games. He was recently diagnosed with Asperger's Syndrome, and is trying to figure out how it affects his writing.